CIVIL WAR

CIVIL WAR

Thomas Adamson, England 1643–1650

by Vince Cross

While the events described and some of the characters in this book may be based on actual historical events and real people, Thomas Adamson is a fictional character, created by the author, and his story is a work of fiction.

Scholastic Children's Books
Commonwealth House, 1–19 New Oxford Street,
London, WC1A 1NU, UK
A division of Scholastic Ltd
London ~ New York ~ Toronto ~ Sydney ~ Auckland
Mexico City ~ New Delhi ~ Hong Kong

Published in the UK by Scholastic Ltd, 2002

Copyright © Vince Cross, 2002

ISBN 0 439 99424 1

1650

My name's Thomas Adamson, and I'll try to tell faithfully what I've seen and heard these past seven or more years of bitter war and trouble. I don't say it's the absolute truth, for there are many kinds of truth, but it's the truth as I believe it. By chance or God's intending I've seen tragedies and disasters the length and breadth of lovely England throughout this time. My various journals and my vivid memories I now combine in the telling of a great and awful story. This is how my benefactor King Charles came to his death on the scaffold in London's Whitehall.

I saw his courage, and I was subject to his tricks, but to this day I do not know if the King was truly a great man or not. Perhaps he even deserved his terrible fate.

You must judge for yourself.

I was born in Grafton Regis in the county of Northamptonshire on 15th August 1630. Forgive me, for I'm sure you know, but the Latin word "Regis" means "of the King". The house in which I spent my childhood belonged to him, though he never came there and I met him only when the house had gone.

Before I was born, my father Simon, steward to Sir Francis and Lady Crane, was thrown from his horse in the great park of Grafton near the Pury Lodge where we lived. He died two days later in my mother's arms. Worried that Sarah (for that was my mother's name) might miscarry the unborn child (me!), Lady Crane took pity and brought her to the graceful galleries and grand rooms of Grafton House to be her companion. She liked my mother for her youth and her infectious giggle.

"It does me good to hear you laugh, Sarah," Dame Mary would say. "Won't you sing for us tonight?"

My mother sang beautifully. The rudest ballads and songs of the court were all the same to her. She was 30 years younger than her mistress, but she reminded Dame Mary of what *she'd* been when she first married Sir Francis: slim waist, long dark hair, and a teasing way with words.

I don't remember the old man very well. He visited rarely. Sir Francis was a gentleman of the past style, very stiff and severe, although he could smile when he wished and he liked children, perhaps because none of his own were left alive. Wheeling and dealing at King Charles's court in London had brought Sir Francis Crane wealth and reputation, but now he lived for literature, for music, for art … and for tapestry. It had been his passion when he and Dame Mary lived at Mortlake, a few miles to the south-west of London, and it stayed that way in remote rural Northamptonshire. So much was this true, that he provided for two boys to be kept in the house at Grafton as apprentices under the watchful eyes of old Josiah Bewley, learning the art and craft of tapestry: wood, wool, warp and weft, cartoon, colour and composition.

The boys would be under Sir Francis's gaze too, when he was there and could spare the time from his great building project at Stoke Park, up the road towards Northampton. If I'd not been all fingers and thumbs, then decorating Stoke in blazing colours might have been my calling too. I might have been one of those apprentices. Josiah tried me out, but it was no use. I've always had an eye for beauty of line and balance in a picture, but not the least talent for making things.

When I was five, Sir Francis, having been perfectly well all his life, was suddenly taken ill with a stomach complaint. The doctors purged him repeatedly, then shook their heads. He was dead within the month. From that moment, my mother became even more important in Dame Mary's life. They'd both lost a husband before their time.

I was left to spend my young childhood doing things no truly well-born boy should have been allowed to do. I ran wild on the ridge where grey-stoned Grafton looked out over the valley of the River Tove, got dirty and wet, was spanked soundly, and then got dirty and wet all over again.

The great house and village were at the end of a promontory that rises a full 150 feet above the river. By the church of St Mary, at the ridge's end, you could climb a tree to see the ground slope away on three sides. On the fourth side, to the west, the land was flat into the park, over and away to Whittlebury forest. It's a fine, airy place to live, and healthy too, or so my mother always said. At that time a good twenty or so of us lived in the house, though most were servants, and a hundred or two more in the village.

Grafton was always for the King, and for the old religion. Over in puritan Northampton they'd have said the incense and bells in St Mary's church, the fine linen in which the parson dressed, the chanting Dame Mary loved, the screen in front of the altar, were all signs of Popish practices. To us they were just natural.

I'd been taught that during noble Queen Elizabeth's reign, all England was one and the same, united under a great ruler. Every book and every scholar said so. Suddenly, while I was yet a small boy, things changed. Now the talk was all that some were for Parliament, and some for the King. It was confusing to know who was on which side. Did it make *so* much difference exactly how you said your prayers? What had the King done to offend people so? If he was King, didn't he have the right to tell people what to do? No one would ever give me clear answers.

There were rumours of families with two brothers where one had declared for each side. When I was about ten, I remember Dame Mary gossiping to my mother that she knew for certain William Anstey from Cambridge spoke on behalf of Parliament while his elder brother Simon was a rising star in the King's service. Dame Mary further said that the Ansteys had *planned* it that way so that if it came to fighting, the family fortune should be secure, whichever side should prevail. I thought to myself how glad I was to be an only child. How terrible to have to fight a brother! I didn't think I could do it.

I got my education from Parson Bunning. Dame Mary and my mother would whisper to each other, thinking that I couldn't hear them.

"He's so bright-eyed, your Thomas!"

"If he paid more attention to his books, he might do better, ma'am."

"Are you sure you're not too hard on him, Sarah?"

"Not hard enough. He has no father, nor in truth has ever had one. I must always be both parents."

"There's Parson Bunning. And Josiah."

At which I can remember my mother raising an eyebrow, and Dame Mary laughing.

Parson Bunning wasn't so very old, and not so boring, and the tasks he set us in Latin and Greek weren't hard for me. We read stories of battles from thousands of years ago, and legends of gods and monsters, and these he made come alive in the cosy library at the end of the house. John Poynter, who was taught with me, found the work more difficult. John was more interested in Scripture than I was. A lot more interested! To tell the truth, I always thought John very dull. He was the only boy of my age in the house, but try as I might, I could never prod him into taking a risk.

"Let's go and make a raft," I'd say.

"Are you sure?" he'd ask, looking half over his shoulder in case anyone had overheard such a dangerous conversation.

"It'll be great sport," I'd encourage him.

He'd ponder a moment, and then hang back, "I don't think so, Tom. I fancy I have a chill coming on..."

And he'd manufacture a sneeze from nowhere to back up his story, sneaking back into the corner with his Latin primer.

He was constantly afraid of being in Dame Mary's bad books, as he was her nephew, and would never try any game or adventure that might carry him there. I always thought he might become a parson himself in time.

"It's good to have John here," I once overheard Dame Mary saying confidentially to my mother.

"Ah, yes," my mother replied. "John..."

"As company for Thomas..." her Ladyship fished.

"John's such a good boy. A steadying influence, wouldn't you say?"

"Quite so, ma'am."

My mother knew what I thought of John, and *I* knew she shared my opinion. She had the same sense of humour and devilment as me.

Josiah Bewley always showed me great good humour. He was with Sir Francis at Mortlake, where famous and highly praised tapestries had been made. He knew everything about the skills of tapestry, and there was nothing he hadn't once been able to create, though at about this time his sight was beginning to ail and his fingers were becoming gnarled and knotted.

As I said, my hands were always unsteady and I couldn't draw to save my life, which made him sad, or so Josiah said. When I was eleven, the last apprentices to live at Grafton left the house for employment elsewhere, though Sir Francis's money maintained a small school of tapestry in Mortlake. These last pupils had made him sad too, Josiah repeatedly told me. In fact, all his apprentices had disappointed him. Not one would ever produce work beyond the ordinary. It wasn't true. He was a great teacher as well as a great craftsman.

In his later years he amused himself with a little

tapestry of his own, and tended the plate and pictures of the house, which he explained to me lovingly. There was a likeness of the playwright William Shakespeare of which he was always very fond, painted on wood. He re-framed it twice to my certain knowledge, and seemed to believe it the most valuable thing in the house. Dame Mary didn't agree.

"I have seen Shakespeare's plays done, Josiah," I once heard her say. "Too bawdy and rude by half."

"Yes, ma'am."

"And he looks too much pleased with himself, don't you think?"

"I don't know about that, ma'am."

"Anyway, it doesn't suit the entrance. He leers at visitors as they arrive. I think it most off-putting. Find somewhere upstairs. A guest room?"

The house at Grafton was very handsome, more than twenty rooms in two storeys of grey and honeyed stone, topped by a roof of Collyweston slate. There were two sets of kitchens, one at the house's east end, and one in a separate block. At the west end were the stables and the village.

Grafton was an old house, first built before Henry VIII came to the throne and thus very long and thin. There were no corridors, as in great buildings of this present day. Since there was just one room's width from north to south, every room opened on to every other, and everyone knew everyone else's business. The stairs were set in two towers at the rear, and the entrance was to the south, on the same side as the large windows which made the house sunny and warm.

Grafton was very dear to Dame Mary. She thought it the most impressive house between Towcester and Northampton, and so it probably was. Only Ashton, three miles across the valley where Alice lived, might have rivalled it.

Alice is a Montagu, distantly related to that rich and famous family which has its seat at Boughton House, though you'd never have known by her bearing that her great-uncles lived in palaces. In 1643, Alice was eleven years old, nearly twelve, and though I might then have been ashamed to say it because she was a girl, Alice was my best friend.

We'd met two summers previously. I'd escaped the Parson's clutches on a hot afternoon, and wandered off down the river towards Ashton. There's a wood down there where the leaves and branches crowd together very densely in high summer. As I passed by, there was a slithering and cracking of twigs high to my right, and a bare-footed, freckle-faced person slid to the ground and stood challenging me, as if she were Maid Marian of Robin Hood's band.

"I'm Boadicea," she said. "Who are you?"

"Scapula?" I said, racking my brains to remember which Roman general it was Queen Boadicea had fought near Watling Street fifteen hundred years ago. The arrow-straight Roman road lay no more than two miles away across the park.

"Honorius Scapula!" I recovered myself. "More than a match for any British queen!"

"*Very* good!" said Alice. "So where do we fight, then?"

Alice often liked to be Boadicea and it suited her very well. She had flame-red hair and a temper to match. What Alice wanted, she always seemed to get. Gradually I became welcome at Ashton and she almost a part of Grafton's family. This was very strange, because as we were for the King, so were the Montagus for Parliament. There was a great difference between the houses, yet it didn't seem to matter.

We played at being Romans and Britons many times and we played Saxons and Normans too (especially at Alderton on the north side of the great park, around the old castle). But we also played Cavaliers and Roundheads without falling out. Alice used to tease me mercilessly.

"When are you going to grow your hair, Cavalier?" she would shout.

"When you cut yours, Roundhead girl," I'd holler back. "Don't you know it's a sin to leave it so? You'll need to stay longer at your prayers tonight!"

We got into trouble sometimes, and our ears boxed, or worse. There was an awkward moment when Alice had the idea that we should take sanctuary in St Mary's church. We were being pursued by a horde of murdering Norman knights, snapping at our heels. It was nip and tuck whether we'd reach safety in time.

We burst in through the south door laughing and shouting, and it took a few moments for us to notice Parson Bunning at his prayers behind the screen. Generally speaking he wasn't a man quick to anger.

This time was different. He sat us down on a hard bench and lectured us with a wagging finger.

"This is a holy place. The sacrament is here. Jesus' body."

Alice wriggled her disagreement beside me.

"In church, everything should be done decorously. Properly. Do you understand, Thomas?"

"Yes, sir," I mumbled.

"And you, Alice, do you understand this also?"

There was an ominous silence.

16

"Do you understand what I'm saying, young lady?" The Reverend Bunning's voice was harsh.

Still Alice said nothing. Finally, in the hanging silence, she could contain herself no longer.

"Well, Jesus isn't really in the bread and wine, *is* he?" she said scornfully.

The Parson looked shocked.

"How *can* he be?" she went on. "It's impossible!"

Parson Bunning's face went purple-red, and he cleared his throat noisily. He was clearly very angry. His eyes flashed as he spoke.

"What you're saying is blasphemy, Alice, although perhaps you have the excuse of ignorance. You may have no one to teach you properly. But when you are in this house, you would do well to respect our way of doing things."

He turned to me.

"Thomas, you and I shall talk of this again soon. On our own."

There was a menace in his voice I'd never heard before. Alice scowled.

"He's going to warn you off me," said Alice, when we were outside.

"Why?" I asked.

"We Montagus are everything he hates."

17

"Why?"

"He's going to lose his living at St Mary's. They're going to throw him out. He's a Papist."

Now I was shocked.

"Who'll throw him out? And how do you know? He's not a Papist. No more than you or me. I've never heard him mention the Pope."

She shrugged.

"I've heard my father speak of it. Soon, he'll be visited and then he'll have no more rights in St Mary's than you or I. Don't worry!" she added, seeing my anxious expression. "I won't tell anyone what happened today, even if the Bunny Rabbit is a spoilsport."

And she pulled her teeth over her lips and made a chomping sound like a rabbit eating grass. It was true, the Parson's teeth were a little prominent. I laughed, and we were friends again.

The day I was thirteen, in August 1643, my mother persuaded Master Peter Aston, who managed the estate's sheep, to have himself and four men of the village make a five-gun salute of celebration. They fired off their pieces at exactly seven in the morning across from the house and opposite my bedroom window. For her pains, my mother was roundly scolded by Dame Mary, who just for a moment thought war had broken out, and that we'd all be taken in chains to the Tower of London that instant. My mother put on a most devoutly sorry expression for Her Ladyship, who couldn't keep from laughing more than a few seconds afterwards, for all that she pretended to be cross.

Maybe it wasn't a very tactful present for my mother to have devised. Of late, we'd begun to understand that it might come to fighting, even at sleepy Grafton. By the middle of 1643, Northampton had been garrisoned by Parliament's men (or the "Roundheads" as we rudely called them) for nearly a year or more, and that was ten miles' distance across the fields. Even a child could leave Grafton in the morning by the back paths, be beside All Saints Church in the centre of Northampton at noon and return by mid-afternoon. It really wasn't very far.

Yet the King's court was at Oxford, and that was just 40 miles the other way from Grafton by a straight and open road. Banbury, also strongly for the King, was even nearer. We were pitched halfway between the two sides. Nevertheless my mother remained confident we'd be safe.

"It's a quarrel that doesn't concern us," she used to say.

I might have been little more than a child, but I was never so sure, and suffered more than once from nightmares in which I was chased by swordsmen and savage dogs. Once I woke screaming to find my mother's anxious expression hovering above me as I lay, the worry-lines in her face heightened by the candle she held. She smoothed back my hair and shushed me back to sleep as if I were a baby.

The last Saturday afternoon in September that year, a small group of men came riding towards Grafton along the road from Northampton. A golden late-autumn

20

sun shone on Alice and me as we watched them from our camp on Low Field. It made the thunder clouds hanging above that town a deep purple-blue, the colour of an angry bruise. Against the sky, the grass around us seemed more green than was possible, Alice's hair a glossy and brilliant beech red.

The riders checked their horses' slow, rolling gait and turned them in towards the house.

"What do they want with Grafton?" I wondered idly.

"Let's see!" said Alice, jumping up.

Running across the ridge and furrow of the fields, we were already behind the wall of the stables as they arrived in the house's main yard. They dismounted stiffly, pulling documents from a pannier.

"Trouble!" said Alice. "I know *him*."

She stabbed a finger in the direction of the tallest man. He was gaunt and grey from one end to another. Grey cloak, grey breeches, grey hair and a grey face.

"His name's Phillips. A *very* important fellow in the Northampton Committee. He's more or less run the town this last three-month, according to Father."

"Why are they here, Alice?" I asked, fearfully.

"Official business, don't you think, Tom? See those parchments. Come to raise taxes from you Grafton people, I shouldn't wonder."

Over the past weeks, there'd been conversation and rumour aplenty about which village had been visited by one side or the other. Money had been demanded, cattle or sheep seized as if by right, men billeted as they pleased, the King's army behaving no better than the Northampton Militia.

We crept in through the back of the house and, making our way through the kitchens, stationed ourselves behind the door that led on to the hall. It hung very slightly open. There we heard the deputation announce themselves. After a moment's silence, Dame Mary's voice sang out very clear and steady. If she was at all frightened, it didn't show.

"Your business, sirs?" she asked.

"Not with you, ma'am, but with your chaplain. The Parson Bunning."

"And if he can't be found?"

"Then we'll make search for him. With your permission."

The last was dishonestly spoken. We'd counted five of them, not armed as far as we could see from across the paddock, but they were large men. They'd do what they wished.

"There'll be no harm to the reverend gentleman. Just something that must be said to him." The man's tone was a little more gentle.

"Regarding?"

"His duties, ma'am."

We heard a single pair of footsteps approach from the drawing room. Alice peered round the crack in our door, and whispered back at me, "It's the Rabbit…"

I put a finger to my lips. This was no time for laughter. Beyond the door, there was the clearing of a throat. A dull voice established that it was in the presence of the Parson, and then began to read dull and legal words with great deliberation. It was hard to make out what was said, because the reader's voice dropped at the end of every monotonous sentence. When he'd finished, there was silence. We held our breath. Any movement from our side might see us discovered. Finally, we heard the Parson's voice, raised and agitated.

"By whose authority do you prevent me from my calling?"

"That of the true Church, sir, which demands a return to the preaching of the Gospel."

"And my Lord Bishop?"

"Not consulted, sir."

"Nor will be?"

"Nor will be."

"In which case," said the Rabbit, his voice stronger still, "I cannot recognize your right to keep me from administering grace and sacrament to the people of this village."

"In which case, Parson, your safety and continuing presence in this place may not be guaranteed."

We watched the visitors go a few minutes later, in the direction they'd come, walking their horses smugly back to Northampton. And a week later, as Alice had predicted, they took the Parson Bunning's living from him. Their own man was appointed in his place, and though my good teacher stayed on with us at Grafton under Dame Mary's safekeeping, the church of St Mary was henceforth out of bounds to him. The new man, Couch, may have been a great preacher. No one knew, because no one went to hear him.

Alice was so often wise for her years. One day in the middle of October, as she swung from a low branch, her skirts muddied and unladylike, she said, "It may be we'll stop being friends for a while, Tom."

I must have looked dismayed, because she added quickly, "But not yet. I'm just saying … it's in the way

24

of things. We're growing up. No mere girl will interest you. You'll have greater things to attend to."

I didn't know whether she was teasing me or not.

She jumped off her swing, and looked me straight in the eye. "Don't look so serious, Tom. But who knows that we shall be friends again much later. At least, I hope so!"

I blushed. "We'll always be friends, Alice! You know we will."

And she ran away shouting, "And one day you'll be able to run faster than me, too!"

A day or so later, Peter Aston met me when I'd finished in the Parson's study and said quietly, "It's time you learned to shoot, Thomas Adamson."

I was surprised. "Am I grown enough, Peter?" I asked. I wasn't much over five foot tall.

"Probably not," he replied, smiling, and looking me up and down, "But you ought to know how it's done! A bit of practice and you'd be a crack shot. I've seen you with a bow and arrow. You've a good eye and steady hands."

We went into the park, by the old hermitage, the two of us and his musket, not much short of five foot long itself.

"Drop the powder in there," said Peter, offering the

barrel towards me. He handed me the scouring stick. "And tamp it down with that."

He produced some lead balls from his jacket pocket, and ran them round the palm of his hand. "Choose your luck!"

I'd seen him making shot by the old barn, carefully pouring white-hot metal into the small moulds. I chose the smoothest, the most perfect, and it too went down the barrel and out of sight, followed by the wadding that would hold the shot in place.

"These things have got a kick like a donkey," remarked Peter about the musket. "This first time, you line her up, but let me take the strain against my shoulder."

The musket was heavy too, more than I could have coped with, and as I pulled the trigger on his command, I wasn't prepared for the ear-splitting report and the explosion which rocked us backwards, so that we both fell over in a tangle of legs. We might have hit the moon, for all I knew. An unmistakable female voice, hollering across the field, broke in on our laughter. I turned round, surprised to see my mother holding up her skirts, running pell-mell across the field.

"What exactly do you think you're doing, Peter Aston?" she shouted as she drew close. "I'll thank you to let me know when you decide to turn my Thomas into a soldier."

I was embarrassed. "It's all right, Mother," I muttered.

"It is *not* all right!" she blazed. "Keep your counsel, and get you home."

I caught Peter Aston's wink as I stomped off towards the house, my mother's voice still bending his ear for his presumption and lack of thought. For all that she was telling him off, I suspected my mother of being sweet on Peter.

"Let's try again next week," he said, as he passed me in the yard next day. And we did, though further away across the park.

That same week I was at Ashton with Alice when her father, Sir Ralph Montagu, came in from Northampton loudly demanding ale and something to eat.

"It's King Charles's young man," he said, as he sat himself down opposite me, smiling.

"I am indeed, sir," I replied, greatly daring.

"I know. Maybe in time you'll see sense."

"I shouldn't think so, sir," I ventured.

He turned to Alice. "There's as much spirit running in his blood as in yours. It must be a catching disease!"

She pulled a face. A thought struck me, and I spoke again, more uncertainly.

"So tell me, sir. Why are you against His Majesty? What wrong has he ever done you? Don't you believe he rules us by God's will?"

He looked at me sideways, sizing me up. For a moment I was concerned I might have gone too far.

"The Parson's still at Grafton, then?"

"Not at the church, sir."

"But evidently in the house!"

He was still teasing, but then stopped himself and became more serious. He leaned forwards and spoke more softly.

"Thomas, you're old enough to know that none of this is easy. Be careful of those who tell you there's nothing but black and white in the world. You're right, I'm not for the King ... but only after a great deal of heart-searching."

Alice's father leaned back, and pushed the hair from his face. He even looked a little melancholy.

"He put aside Parliament, you know ... wouldn't let them meet, because they dared refuse him money to fight battles he should never have started against the Spanish and the Scots. Now did the good Parson tell you that?"

As far as Parson Bunning was concerned, most of England was faithless and ungrateful because they quarrelled with King Charles. Especially Parliament. If the King wanted money, he should have it.

"Is the King a Papist, sir?"

Ralph Montagu looked very hard at me.

"I don't know what's in his heart, Tom. I can't tell you whether the King looks to the Pope or not for his orders. I only know what he *does*. He's arrested good men who've opposed him, like Sir John Eliot. Some of them died. And he married a Catholic."

"They say Henrietta Maria was very pretty," chirped up Alice.

Her father turned to her. "Do they, whoever *they* may be? Pretty is as pretty does in a queen, as in any woman!"

"But how may it be right to raise arms against a king?" I pressed him.

"Let me answer your question with another, Tom. Is it *ever* justified to raise arms against another?"

"If your wife was threatened, sir. Or your daughter?"

I looked at Alice, who was pretending to be very bored.

"True, Tom. That's what men commonly say. But some of us believe that this king threatens the lives of all in England. He may be a tyrant in the making." He leaned back in his chair and wagged a finger.

29

"Though of course there are many lining their pockets through the mayhem of this war. There's looting and pillage and it's a scandal! Remember what I told you, Tom! Nothing's black or white. Just pray you're not required to choose between the two sides, when you may feel for neither."

I was struck by what Sir Ralph Montagu said, and young as I was, I sensed bitterness in those last words. There was no one like him at Grafton for bearing and argument. I respected and liked Parson Bunning, but he was blind to any but his own opinion.

The next day, with October drawing to a close, Alice and I went out of the great park towards the castle keep at Alderton.

There were only a few lumps of stone still left standing around the grassy mound. The rest had been robbed away long ago to build houses and barns around the village. The top of the mound was quite flat inside. Tables could be laid and a party in full swing, and no one in the park would have known it. Trees kept it secret from the outside world, which was why Alice and I liked the castle so much.

As we came close, we could see a slim column of smoke rising from inside.

"Travellers?" said Alice.

"Or soldiers?" I guessed.

Quietly and carefully, we pulled ourselves up the bank, screening ourselves from what might lie beyond by the bushes and trees. As we peered over the top, we saw about a dozen cavalrymen and their horses spread around the grass. The men were relaxed, chatting and pulling on clay pipes. Their helmets and armour lay beside them. Water was boiling in a pot over the fire.

"The King's men or Parliament's?" I whispered to Alice.

She shrugged. I'd learned from Peter Aston that sometimes there was no way of telling unless you knew the field signs soldiers wore — a piece of paper, a plume, a sash. "They say there's many a man been killed by his own," Peter had said darkly.

"Who wants to know? That's the question!" said a voice in the tree above us. We jumped in surprise. As we watched, we found we were being watched in turn.

"Not spies then, are you?" said the man in the tree, shimmying down the trunk and jumping the last five feet or so. He was short and well-built, not an obvious shape for a fighting man, though he moved easily considering the size of his stomach.

"No, sir!" I answered quickly. There were butterflies dancing inside me, but I wasn't going to let him know.

"We're from the village over the park."

"Grafton?" he asked.

I nodded, swallowing hard.

"Then since you ask, we're Corporal Thorogood and his company, who are pleased to serve the King and Prince Rupert under Sir John Digby." He looked so proud and puffed-up as he said this. I decided at once I didn't like him.

He paused, stroking his chin, play-acting at deep thought. "But how do I *know* you're not spies? You could betray our position as soon as my back's turned."

I thought it was probably his idea of a jest, but being not absolutely certain, I was for the moment tongue-tied.

"You could ride back with us, if you wanted," said Alice innocently, coming to the rescue. "Then you'd know."

From the corner of my eye, I caught movement in the camp behind the soldier. His companions were pulling on their swords, tightening their belts, stamping on the fire, making rapid preparations to move on. One of them let out a long low whistle in the direction of our captor. He made a signal of acknowledgement.

"I must go! And remember, *never* play near soldiers, children. Any more than you would a swarm of bees!

Understand?" This warning was spoken fiercely. I was hurt to be referred to as "children" in front of Alice. My ears burned.

"Stupid man," said Alice, when he'd gone off at the double. " 'Don't play near soldiers!' Who does he think we are?"

In two minutes or less, the whole troop had picked up their baggage and ridden out from Alderton. They went at a quiet trot rather than a noisy gallop, as if they wished not to draw attention to themselves.

"I want to know what made them strike camp all of a sudden," I said.

"We'll be able to see from over there, whatever it is," Alice replied.

From the north side of the castle keep there was a good view towards Northampton. In the lane that stretched out that way, we could make out a score of other men on horseback, moving slowly towards us.

"Do you think it's the Northampton Militia?" breathed Alice. "If it is, there'll be a fight, for sure!" She seemed pleased at the idea, as if it were another game that we played. I was cross with her.

"A fight in which someone might be killed," I snapped. "Perhaps even the man we just met. This isn't Normans and Saxons any more, Alice!"

She went silent and sulky on me.

"I'm sorry," I said, instantly regretting the way in which I'd spoken.

It had been a dry autumn, and the lanes were still dusty, so when the small troop of King's men emerged from the lee of the hill below us and galloped towards the oncoming soldiers, they raised a cloud behind their hooves, though the cloud was hidden from the Parliamentary force by the hedges along the lane. When they were perhaps half a mile apart, the Militia finally saw the enemy bearing down on them, shouting and firing pistols. For a moment there was confusion and indecision. Those in front halted momentarily. A couple of horses took fright, nearly pitching their riders into the ditches. In the instant, some riders moved forward, and others seemed to think of retreating.

As far as I could see, the Militia didn't seem to return fire. I knew muskets were useless from the saddle, but why weren't they using their pistols? Perhaps they had none. When the King's men were almost upon them, the Roundheads threw their horses around and retreated towards Northampton as fast as they could, throwing up a new screen of dust in the face of the oncoming cavalry. The King's horse chased for a short distance, but then gave up. So did we, and we returned excitedly to Grafton to report the first skirmish in our district, which ended without casualties on either side.

When you have a good story to tell, it's very aggravating to find that someone has a better one. We came into the old house at Grafton to find the household and village already very agitated. General Sir Philip Skippon was a man who'd gained great reputation on Parliament's side and the previous day he'd made the town of Newport Pagnell his, according to Anthony Smith, the innkeeper, who'd just visited his brother there. Newport was nearer to Grafton than Northampton, perhaps only six miles to the south-east across the fields.

Dame Mary had also heard from her good friend Frances Abthorpe that Prince Rupert was now in Towcester with a great Royalist force, just half a dozen miles across Watling Street in the *other* direction. The general opinion was that the cavalry Alice and I had seen were a scouting party sent out from Rupert's main body of troops.

So we were now between the two foes, and the worry was widely expressed that in a land generally criss-crossed with hedges and ditches, the open land of Grafton's great park would make a good battlefield.

The Parson was holding up a Roundhead news sheet

which Anthony Smith had brought back with him. He read it to whoever would listen:

"The enemy around Towcester…" (they meant by this the King's men!) "…drive the fields of all cattle. Poor Northamptonshire, especially to the west, as you have been faithful to the Parliament, so have your miseries been great. What your reward hereafter may be, God knows!"

The Parson shook his head in disgust. As he balled up the paper he said venomously, "What weasel words! Is not Parliament the chief despoiler of men's livelihoods?" He was becoming a more bitter and angry man by the day, driven by his own misfortune. Dame Mary nodded her head in sad agreement.

Just over two weeks later, on the early morning of 15th November, not long after sunrise, a regiment of the King's horse, under Sir John Digby, announced themselves at the front door of Grafton House, and gave Dame Mary to understand that they'd invited themselves to stay for as long as it might be. The stabling at Grafton was excellent, they said, and the position of the house and village, lying astride the main road and with commanding views of the countryside, was excellent for defence.

There was grumbling in the house about the fuss that would be caused, but Sir John assured Dame Mary his men were perfectly behaved, and would conduct themselves so well she wouldn't know they were around her house and on her land. Besides, he said, with the garrison of Parliament now established at Newport, surely she'd rather know she was protected, than at the mercy of thieves and marauders.

My mother found me later, took me by the shoulders, and looked me directly in the eye.

"Things are changing, Tom," she said softly.

"I know *that*, Mother," I said, sounding too sure of myself. "I've been telling you so for weeks."

"Don't be so cocky, my lad!" she snapped, eyes flashing. "You know no more than I how it will go for us."

I saw her temper was a sign of her deep concern, and said I was sorry.

"What I mean to say is that the arrival of Sir John marks us," she went on. "Of course this house was always for the King, yet we have never thought to shout it from the church tower!"

"Perhaps it's better we wear our colours boldly?" I suggested. I didn't know whether I believed this, but I suppose I said it to test the idea.

"You'll no longer be safe roaming the countryside unprotected."

"I won't come to any harm."

"Musket fire isn't *so* accurate, Tom. Shots go astray, and find all kinds of unintended targets. Young men and boys included. I hope Peter's taught you that much at least!"

I blushed. I was inclined to underestimate what my mother knew.

"And Alice is now a daughter of the enemy, from Sir John Digby's point of view…"

A hot-cold sensation caught me at the back of the neck. Ralph Montagu's words echoed in my ears. *"Just pray you're not required to choose between two sides,"* he'd said.

A choice was being made for me, against my will. Alice was to be out of bounds. She'd known it might happen.

"I'm sorry…" my mother said gently, seeing how upset I was at losing my best friend. "Truly I'm sorry. But better you hear it from me than anyone else."

I managed to sneak out to see Alice just twice more in the weeks that followed. The first time I confided in my mother that I intended to go to Ashton. I said I'd slip out at dawn over the the garden. Who was to know I wasn't up early to collect wood or mushrooms?

"At least ride there," she said.

"Riskier than walking," I answered back. "The soldiers don't like the back paths. They can't see what's round the next corner."

"Well, leave yourself good time to be back before dark! Be careful Tom," she shouted as I went through the door.

To be truthful, seeing Alice wasn't much fun. The nights were drawing in, the days were becoming just about as short as days can be, and the weather had become true November at last, foggy and damp. Stuck inside the gloomy house at Ashton we couldn't find much to talk about that didn't set us arguing.

From being a backwater, Grafton had become a centre of attention overnight. There seemed to be hundreds of the King's men, infantry and cavalry, all over the village, some days more, some days less. They came in cheerfully during the morning from Towcester, and returned to their base as late as might be safe. There was a danger of ambush by the Militia, so maybe 200 or more slept where they could around the village, in houses and barns.

The plan seemed to be to secure the three sides of the slope around the house and church from attack. The Monday before Advent, towards the end of November, I watched as the men built shallow turf banks, reinforcing them from time to time with more solid firing posts, where they built the bank higher and backed it with stone. They swore loudly as they grazed their hands and knees digging out stone from one place and carrying it to another. I wanted to help but they laughed as I tried to lift the long slices of turf they threw about with such freedom. I couldn't shift them an inch.

The north terrace that Dame Mary called the "gallery" became a favourite place for the soldiers, despite her complaints. They liked what she'd liked: the uninterrupted view of the valley.

"If anyone comes at us from there," said one mud-spattered infantryman, "we'll cut them down, like *that*." He snapped his fingers in relish.

I learned that the church was easy to defend for the same reason. A fight up from the river would go unrewarded. You didn't need to be a general to work it out. The ground was waterlogged and overlooked by the steep hill.

"They'll come at us from the west, across the flat," said the soldier, pointing beyond the village at the lovely park where kings had once hunted. He spat loudly. "And we'll be ready for them!"

They concentrated the main body of troops in the V-shape made by the two village lanes that ran out to the main Northampton road from the church, using the buildings that lined that road as cover. Since this included Anthony Smith's alehouse amongst other dwellings, a steady stream of moans and groans from villagers found their way to Dame Mary. She listened to them as sympathetically as she could. I heard her talking to Anthony Smith and Josiah.

"What can I do, Anthony?" she said, spreading her hands. "You see what they've done to the gallery? Years of work ruined!"

"They've no respect, ma'am," complained Josiah. "Sir Francis would have given them what for, and no mistake!"

Dame Mary looked downcast. There were times she missed her husband very much.

Communication with Alice had become really difficult now. One Friday I persuaded Peter Aston, who was riding over that way, to leave a note for her saying I'd call early the next morning.

It was a crisp clear day and the winter's first ice was on the puddles in the cart ruts. Alice and I practised with our bows for an hour, laughing, competing hard to be the best. If anything, although she couldn't shoot as far, Alice's aim was better than mine.

As we said goodbye, she caught my hand. She'd never done that in all the time I'd known her. It was something grown-ups did. We were just friends, that was all.

"Tom, I'm afraid for you," she said.

"You don't have to be. Think of those soldiers around us every night."

"That's why I'm afraid. You'd be better off almost anywhere else."

The thought of leaving Grafton had genuinely never entered my head. I was shocked.

"We couldn't do that!" I said. "Where would we go, Mother and I?"

"My father would lodge you and your mother here. I know he would." Alice's eyes lit up.

"Mother would never leave Dame Mary," I answered. It was true.

"No, I don't suppose she would," said Alice quietly. "Well anyway, take care!" And for a brief second or two she threw her arms around me and hugged me. Then she ran inside without looking back, and I was left to walk home feeling confused and most unlike myself.

I hadn't gone a quarter of a mile when I saw a band of infantry approaching from the south-east on the far side of the Tove. My heart thumped. They were just a dozen, but their careful plodding march from the direction of Newport Pagnell made me think they might be Roundheads. I certainly didn't recognize any of the soldiers as being from our garrison at Grafton. They seemed to be on reconnaissance, pointing this way and that at the angles of the fields and the width of the river. They were quietly and systematically noting the lie of the land, seeing where it was passable and where a band of soldiers might find themselves trapped by the thicket. I shadowed them for a quarter of an hour or more, making a mental picture of everything they did. Here was my chance to make an impression with Sir John Digby. I might only have been a boy whose muscles weren't yet strong enough to haul stones and turf, but my brain was sharp.

When I'd seen enough, I doubled back to Grafton, half-scuttling along the ground at first, trying to slip into the grounds of the house beside the church without any fuss. Instead I ran straight into the stout cavalryman who'd made my ears burn so at Alderton. Inwardly I cursed my luck.

"Well, well, so we meet again," he crowed. "I thought I told you to stay away from soldiers!" His tone was almost a sneer.

"I live here," I said firmly.

"So you do. I'd forgotten that." He'd done no such thing! He barred my way.

"So where have you been?" he asked, challengingly.

44

"Is it your business?" I replied, rudely. I was cross.

"Everything that goes on around Grafton's our business."

"I've been to see a friend." I tried to keep my dignity and not let my voice shake.

"Oh, have you? And who might that be?" He paused, enjoying my embarrassment, spinning it out. It was as if an innocent thought had suddenly dropped into his mind. "Perhaps the pretty little girl with red hair? Your sweetheart?" he sneered.

Once more his manner was such as to suggest that everything about us was silly and childlike. He really was most unpleasant.

"If you mean Alice Montagu, then yes," I said, "but far more important than where I've been is the information I have." I spelled it out. "*Military* information!"

"Don't try to wriggle off the hook," he said. "You shouldn't be out, and you know it. Especially not visiting Montagus. Don't cover your tracks with cock and bull stories!"

It was no use. Maybe he'd been picked on that day by his commander, and needed to take it out on someone. I let him continue venting his spleen, and then went on into the house, pretending I did so with my tail between my legs.

Once inside, I pulled myself together, and decided I wouldn't be put off by the pig-ignorance of one disgruntled soldier.

I put pen to paper and, addressing the letter to Sir John Digby, I told about what I'd seen down by the river. I sealed the note, found Dame Mary, explained and asked her what I should do. She seemed amused, although I couldn't see why. But she did say she'd make sure Sir John had the letter by the end of the afternoon.

To my surprise and pleasure I was called to see the great man in Dame Mary's drawing room the next morning. I'd not even shaken his hand before. He was tall and sandy-haired, the hair thin and receding. It gave his face a very open and honest look. He smiled warmly and asked me to sit down. His manner was completely the opposite of his private soldier. He treated me exactly as he would a grown-up, and was most polite.

"I think you're right about the soldiers you saw. They're taking the pulse of the King's army," he said, his eyes narrowing. "And shortly shall find it much alive, I hope."

I nodded.

"You write very well?" It was half a statement, half a question.

"If I do, it's Parson Bunning's work, sir," I replied.

Sir John nodded his approval. "He's a good man, and never deserved his treatment."

Since the arrival of Sir John, the Parson had been restored to the services at St Mary's with full chant, candles and robes. Couch and his long thin face had been set roughly on the road to Northampton with instructions not to come back.

I didn't know what to say. I was rather shy of this imposing man.

"Your father's dead?" he continued.

"I never knew him, sir. He was killed in a riding accident before I was born."

"My sons are far away," he said, rather vaguely. "I trust to God they're safe."

This time my silence prompted him to continue.

"They're soldiers too," said Sir John. "They've been in the north country. Things aren't going so well up there."

He asked how I occupied my time at Grafton, and commented on the quality of the tapestries which blazed in bright colours from the walls. I explained some of the scenes they showed from the country around Grafton and in turn asked him some questions about soldiering. Wasn't it very

47

lonely, to be so far from family? He smiled a faint smile.

"It can be lonely to be in command," he said, and sounded melancholy for a moment. Then he collected himself. "I must be about my business," he said briskly. "Thank you for your intelligence report. You're a bright lad. Keep your eyes open and come and talk to me again soon."

After that, whenever we encountered each other around the house and enclosure, he always stopped to pass the time of day.

However sweet Sir John's promises to Dame Mary about the behaviour of his men, their need to survive the winter cold and make a life for themselves caused problems.

Things arrived in the village that didn't belong there. Word reached Dame Mary's ears that bedding and pots from houses and farms in the locality had been taken to keep the garrison comfortable. Dame Mary told my mother who told me.

"It isn't right!" mother grumbled. "And if I catch a soldier napping on a feather bed in one of our barns, I'll tell him so."

Thinking of the soldiers I'd encountered I said, "Just be careful, won't you? They're not all gentlemen, you know."

She smiled at me. "I can hear your father saying that. I know my quick temper will be the end of me. But it's *not* right, is it?"

It was the kind of thing she often said: "…*my quick temper will be the end of me*…" My beautiful mother was always so quick to speak up against injustice or unkindness. But this time, her resolute words cast a shadow I only understood later on.

By the second week of the month, there were regularly 300 or more men and 200 extra horses within the village limits, according to Peter Aston. Grafton was three times in number the size it had been and, with the miserable weather, everyone was on edge.

The arrival of the artillery caused a stir. Six pieces arrived, one by one from Towcester, struggling through the churned-up mud of the lanes. They were installed on the corners of the defences inside the bulwarks of turf and stone.

"I don't like it," said Peter to me as we rolled dice together. "They expect that we'll be attacked soon or why else would they bring up the big guns?"

A few days later, while the Parson attempted to keep me and John Poynter to the task of translating yet another speech of Cicero to the Roman Senate, there was a sudden commotion outside the house. Someone or something seemed to have touched the soldiers' coarse anger. When we were free, I went to see what had happened. Josiah Bewley was leaning on a wall at the gate of the house, well-wrapped against the bitter weather, sucking on his pipe and looking towards the old hollow way which leads down to the river. A young man, half stripped of his clothes, was manacled to one of a stand of trees, shivering and blue in the sleet that blew in on the wind.

"What's he done?" I asked Josiah, shocked to see such a cruel thing.

"He's a spy," the old man grunted. "So they say."

The boy was out there in the numbing cold all day and, as Peter told me, when they'd learned from him all they believed they could, he was beaten soundly and sent on his way. To look at, he didn't seem a great deal older than me. I felt relieved when I heard he'd been released. I'd been afraid they'd kill him when he'd told his tale and was no longer useful. I shuddered to think what might have happened if the Roundhead soldiers had taken me prisoner that day in November.

XXX

On the morning of 22nd December, a great number of enemy cavalry and foot soldiers passed to the south of Grafton in full view of the house, marching in the direction

51

of Towcester. Mother called to me from upstairs, and together we watched from a window as they marched purposefully along the cattle road in the valley.

"You see!" said my mother triumphantly. "What interest is sweet Grafton to anyone, Sir John Digby or no?"

Out towards the village, the regiment at Grafton made ready, in case a call came to reinforce the Towcester garrison, but no message came.

Then, before dark and to our great surprise, the enemy returned to encircle us in even greater numbers. There were thousands of them in the surrounding countryside, so our scouts said, and mere hundreds of us within the village. For my mother's sake, I dared not show my feelings, but deep inside I was eaten with fear as we watched the enemy troops assemble. Over and over again I imagined what it would be like to have the steel of a rapier run between my ribs. I hoped that when it came, death would come quickly to all those I loved, and that I should be able to show the bravery of a man.

At length, Sir John Digby sent word to those in the house that we should stay within its walls, if we valued our safety. Even then we should keep as far from the windows as possible. We dragged ourselves away from our vantage points in the bedrooms and settled on the north side of the downstairs rooms closest to the stairwells.

As night began to fall a Roundhead regiment on foot attacked from the south-east across the hollow way where the ancient village of Grafton had once stood. We could hear the reports of their muskets, and louder answering fire from the rooms above us and by the gates. Every discharge echoed down terrifyingly through the stonework.

The men of the house had gone to join in the defence. The rest of us huddled together in the recesses of the house. My mother clung to me, shaking with fear. Dame Mary sat in a chair. She had some sewing with her, and seemed outwardly very calm, her energy going into her dancing fingers, a single candle softly lighting her work.

"They'll never break in," she said, rather too often. "And tomorrow we shall see what happens when our brave soldiers get to work."

"We're all going to die," wailed one of the house-maids, speaking for many of us.

"Nonsense, Tabitha," said Dame Mary resolutely. "Why should anyone wish to kill you? You're far more use alive than dead."

This made Tabitha wail all the louder. Her sobbing rubbed off on one or two of the other kitchen girls, but made the rest of us more determined to show spirit. The gnawing fear I'd felt earlier on had now disappeared, but I found I couldn't keep still. Like a cornered animal, I paced backwards and forwards. What was going on out there in the dark? It was unbearably frustrating not to know, and not to be able to affect whatever was going to happen.

The Parson was there too. He was dignified and brave, talking to those who were distressed and helping practically as he could. He poured ale, and cut bread, though he had no need to wait on anyone. In between, he prayed silently.

In half an hour or so, the shooting stopped, and one of the officers, bluff, red-faced Major Brockbank, stepped in to tell us he thought we were safe until daybreak.

"Do we know who it is we contend with?" asked Dame Mary, stiff and serious.

"We believe the Orange and Green regiments of the London bands under Sir Philip Skippon may have joined with Parliamentary horse from Northampton, ma'am," the Major replied. "I daresay they fancied they could take us by surprise, but they were wrong of course."

"And tomorrow?"

"They'll try again. But the weather's on the turn, and laying siege is little fun in the cold and wet. And we may have reinforcements by then..."

Brockbank was right about the weather. We woke to find cloud hanging low over us, a north wind and rain as cold as it can be short of hail. However, he was wrong about the reinforcements. Our men fought courageously all through that Saturday against musket and artillery fire, but no help came.

"We should be preparing for Christmas," said my mother sadly.

Along with others, soldiers and village men, Peter Aston was at the upstairs windows with his musket, but he took the opportunity of a lull in the firing to see how we were doing down below. It must have been about one o'clock.

"What's happening, Peter?" I asked.

He was excited from the battle, and spoke breathlessly. "There must be a thousand of them," he said.

"Then there's no hope?"

"Don't forget your history books, Master Tom, and all the times a greater force has been sent packing by a lesser."

"Are there many killed?"

"None that I've seen."

"Really?"

"Truthfully. Our muskets just reach them, but with no accuracy. And for the moment they must hope we waste our fire. They'll wait as long as they dare, though not for ever. They'll be afraid Prince Rupert may relieve us. It's said he's somewhere out beyond Towcester towards Weedon."

However, not all Peter's news was good.

"They've moved beyond the main road, Tom, and I can't pretend it's not a setback. The alehouse is taken and the bakery too, along with most of the buildings on the Northampton road. They're bringing in more artillery pieces behind the cover, and may hope to play them on us now."

This seemed very bad news to me, but Peter remained remarkably cheerful. Maybe he was just keeping my spirits up. When he'd disappeared upstairs again, a sense of quiet foreboding settled on us. Waiting was so hard.

In the early afternoon the first low explosions of the big guns could be heard, and a few times the house was jolted to its foundations as the missiles found their mark. But Grafton's walls were solid and thick, and the artillery seemed to do little damage.

They had a greater effect on the people inside. We all began to feel panic. Many of the women were tearful, and a couple of the kitchen girls had completely sunk into themselves. Their faces were white, their expressions blank. From the great number of frightened people in such a confined space and the lack of airing, the house began to smell bad. There were only two or three places such as the library and around the stairs that were safe and unoccupied by our defenders and their baggage. Sir John made sure to keep everyone as calm as he could, sending an officer into the house to check now and again. Once he even came himself, grimy and grim faced.

"Keep your courage, everyone," he said, with as much cheerfulness as he could. "It'll all come right in the end."

I don't think anyone believed him.

The second night of the siege was harder than the first, for food and water were running short. It was all the worse because we knew it was Christmas Eve.

"How long will this go on?" said my mother in

desperation the next morning. "I thought they called themselves Christian men? Will they make a celebration of Christ's birth with gunfire?"

At mid-morning, an unnaturally pale Peter Aston joined us.

"Are you all right, Peter?" asked my mother, looking him over anxiously.

"Not so, Sarah," he answered, sitting down on a stool rather too quickly. "I've just done something I never dreamt of, and that's kill a man."

"How come?" I asked. "How do you know for sure?"

"I shot him from the window and saw him fall," answered Peter. "And he's still lying there with his companions around him. He's dead. I know he is."

I was confused. How could you shoot a musket so well, and be so appalled at the result. Wasn't this what a gun was for?

For a full ten minutes, he sat there shaking his head, his hands trembling, before duty carried him back upstairs. Like all the men, he was becoming exhausted from two days of concentration and fear.

A little later, the enemy assault on the house seemed to redouble. I put my hands to my ears to try to shut out the noise, but it made little difference. Explosion after explosion rocked the walls, and the musket fire above us became more intense. Pictures hung crookedly. Some crockery slipped to the floor in the drawing room next door and smashed. After one loud report, plaster and dust fell from the library ceiling and Tabitha's friend began to scream hysterically. I held on to my mother, and she rocked me in her arms as she'd done when I was small. Even Dame Mary was clearly agitated, knuckles clenched, a muscle in her cheek twitching in spite of herself. It couldn't go on. The house would fall, sooner or later.

Finally Sir John made a last appearance, ghostlike, his hair askew, and asked for silence. There could scarcely be that. The gunfire around us was constant.

"I shall seek a truce," he said, "or this will end disastrously. I shall ask safe passage for all the women and children. Truly, I'm sorry that our wish to serve the King has brought you to this." There was a tear in his eye, which he swiftly wiped away with his torn sleeve. "I thank you all for your consideration and kindness. Wherever I end my days, I'll remember Grafton with affection. Before I go, for my peace of mind, I'd like to hear Parson Bunning say a prayer."

The Parson asked that God would have mercy on us all, and Sir John left us.

In a few minutes there was a short burst of gunfire. Then it stopped all together. I only heard afterwards that the first drummer lad who'd gone to deliver Sir John's message had been shot. He died a day later from his wounds.

The surrender was complete by nightfall. We saw no more of Sir John, nor Major Brockbank, and all the men were taken from the house to the barns outside, even Parson Bunning and Josiah.

At least now we could spread ourselves out around the house, although the Roundheads kept us from going upstairs, at first quite politely. Fresh ale was brought from the kitchens, together with supplies of not quite stale bread. But for the third night we had little sleep, and ached from the winter cold, uneasy in body and mind as we camped on chairs and the floor in the large drawing room.

Things were different the next morning. There were men all over the house, and by the noise overhead, it was clear they were busy looting as they fancied. Their laughter and the sound of splintering and smashing became too much for Dame Mary. For the first time she broke into desperate crying. Everything she and Sir Francis had worked for was being destroyed around her. My mother put an arm about her. I felt hopeless and useless. I was watching as our life was being pulled down around us.

Finally the ruffians tumbled into the drawing room, and it was obvious they intended more mischief.

There were some half-dozen common soldiers, perhaps slightly tipsy for all they were supposedly so high-minded. They entered the room crudely, elbowing us aside. They were as free with the women as with plate. In the sudden confusion I was separated from my mother and I heard her cry out in surprise. When I tried to move, it was as if my legs were held fast by mud in some terrible dream.

I turned and saw her stagger backwards with one of the soldiers pressed lewdly against her. In the act of falling she grabbed a paper knife from the writing table. Her arm arched back and then forward, thrusting the knife at her attacker to make him stop his advance. In the struggle he lost his balance too and pitched forward, collapsing on to the knife with a scream of anguish. Immediately and from close beside him came a pistol shot, deafeningly loud in the crowded room. My mother sagged to the floor.

There was a sudden appalled silence. The room seemed to freeze. I was rooted to the spot, speechless and numb.

Then there was pandemonium. Two officers arrived at the double, drawn by the pistol shot. A man of obvious medical knowledge was there, kneeling beside my mother, tearing at her clothes. The soldiers were cuffed around the face and taken away under guard.

The medical man bent low for several minutes, but finally shook his head. My mother's eyes were closed, the delicate skin of her face a creamy, waxen colour, tinged with blue. She wasn't breathing. I fell forward to where she lay, whispering to her, begging her time and again to wake up. At length they had to tear me from her lifeless body.

Late that afternoon, they sent the women and children out from Grafton and put us down on the road with nothing but what we wore, Dame Mary equally as the humblest chambermaid. The common soldiers and the men of the village were held under guard. We saw them shivering and crestfallen among the shattered outbuildings as we were herded away from the house. The important names were carried away without ado. The Parliamentary soldiers boasted that Sir John Digby was to be sent to the Tower of London: others to lesser prisons. Even the Parson was taken.

As we stumbled away in the twilight of this most bitter Christmas Day, one of the women turned towards

Grafton and let out a howl of despair. The evening sky behind us was an unnatural red. As an example to others, "for the prevention of further inconvenience", the Roundheads had set fire to the great house.

The soldiers of Parliament had killed my mother, and destroyed our lives, and I didn't understand why. I had no feelings and every feeling. I was numb with shock at one moment, a ball of blazing anger at the next. My life as I'd known it was gone: I had lost everything that was precious to me in a single day. And for the first time I knew what it was to hate.

26th December 1643 – February 1644

We all of us passed a dreadful first night at Pury Lodge, the home of my distant childhood, on the far side of the great park. We picked our way along the lane from memory because it was so dark, tripping over ruts and fallen branches. For me it was in truth a nightmare journey. I stumbled along in a daze, my mind still struggling to understand what I'd seen, still reliving the sack of the house and my mother's murder.

We fully expected to meet more soldiers and further abuse when we arrived at the Lodge but the house was empty. Of Philip Partridge, Dame Mary's present steward, whose family home it now was, there was not a sign, nor any of his wife and baby daughter.

The Militia had been there all right. The doors of the Lodge were swinging open and they were pockmarked with shot. Our voices echoed eerily around the empty rooms when we called the Partridges' names. The house had been ransacked.

I was in shock, and shivered my way through the

night. They covered me with what blankets they could find, and in the end I slept, despite the bitter cold. I woke to find Dame Mary watching me. I think she had stayed beside me the whole night long.

The previous months at Grafton I'd begun to think of myself as very nearly a man, but in the next days I returned to being a child, blindly doing as I was told, quite unable to make decisions for myself. Inside, I ached for my mother Sarah, and the ache would never quite go away. Until then I hadn't understood how much I'd loved her. Now every day began with the hope that her death was just a bad dream. And then as I woke properly I'd remember the truth and the gnawing pain would return to my stomach.

Of the fifteen or so women and children who arrived at Pury only five of us went on the few miles towards Towcester the next day – Dame Mary, Tabitha the maid and Rachel her friend, John Poynter and myself. All the others went to relations near by to wait for the hoped-for return of their menfolk.

"Frances will take us in," said Dame Mary, meaning her friend Frances Abthorpe, whose house was on the northern edge of town.

We were welcomed and made comfortable, but within days we were on the move again.

"Now that Grafton's fallen, they think Sir Philip Skippon will try for a bigger prize," said Frances Abthorpe, shaking her grey head. "He has a grudge against Towcester. The town's by no means safe."

Dame Mary looked thoughtful. "Then we'll go to Oxford. Since we've suffered in the King's cause, we'll seek the King's protection."

"What'll you do about Tom?" said Frances. They were talking about me as if I wasn't there.

"I'll write some letters on his behalf," replied Dame Mary. "The name of Sir Francis Crane still means something, I hope."

"To the King himself?" asked Frances, with a look of awe.

"The very same!" Dame Mary said firmly. "What was lost at Grafton can never be replaced, for Thomas or for me. But it was the King's house, and he should know how one of his household has been orphaned."

The word "orphan" was quite familiar to me, but now it fell on my ears like a blow. I had not considered it might apply to me, and my inner loneliness and despair deepened.

Horses and a cart were hired and for two days we fought through the rain and mud to Oxford. When we arrived, I discovered Dame Mary was right. The name of Sir Francis Crane truly could still open doors. We found ourselves in lodgings at the University's lovely Magdalen College, close to the River Cherwell.

Looking back, I can see now what my sorrow hid from me then. It must have been humiliating for Dame Mary to rely on the charity of others. Sir Francis Crane had once been a friend to Magdalen College, she told me firmly. Now it must be a friend to his family in their hour of need. We were cramped and confined in three bare oak-panelled rooms in one of the college courtyards, but we were warm and dry, and there was food.

London had become impossible for King Charles several years ago. He'd moved to a town which was easy to defend, and where the buildings were beautiful. Or so Richard Hardisty said, with his easy laugh, as he leaned back on his chair in Magdalen's gaudily painted hall after dinner. Richard Hardisty was our benefactor in Oxford. He grew up with Sir Francis, fought with him as a boy, drank with him as a young man, and was in business with him until his death. Then he became a fellow of Magdalen College, a man of great learning and presence, tall and dome headed, with remarkably piercing, deep-set eyes, which twinkled or frowned from moment to moment.

To be close to the great town of Oxford and a royal court was an extraordinary change in my life. There were so many large and elegant buildings, handsomely built of finely cut warm stone, lining so many broad and graceful streets, with so many important people in fine clothes strutting busily about them. At first I didn't understand was going on, but I loved being there. I would gaze at the perfect shapes of the windows and towers, and wonder at their balance and proportions.

"You've arrived at a moment of history, young Thomas," Richard Hardisty thundered. His voice was so heavy, *his* side of conversations could always be heard a room or two away.

"Why so, sir?" I asked.

"Finding one Parliament in London not to his taste, the King's fashioning another more to his liking here, though what exactly he has the power to decide upon, I can't imagine." He raised one eyebrow in a way that made me laugh. "But I tell you, it's quite changed Oxford. We used to be such a sleepy little town, debating how many angels could dance upon a pin. Now the King has arrived, flooding fields and throwing up earthworks, half the powerful men of England are busily walking its streets. All those that wouldn't wish to put him in a dungeon!"

"But surely Oxford's pleased to entertain the King?" I suggested.

"I daresay many will tell you it's an excellent idea, while in their hearts wishing him far away," said Richard. "Having a king to stay is always a mixed blessing. Your very best may not be good enough. Kings will take what they want, without understanding the need for payment. So the people of Oxford suffer more than a little. Every working man has to give time to build the earthworks around the garrison, you know. Without payment!"

The cruelty of the Roundheads as I'd experienced it at Grafton made me leap to the King's defence.

"I've seen the work of men who believe themselves beyond a king's authority," I said passionately. "It's destruction and terror. My mother died by their hands. Far better an imperfect king than an impious parliament."

He saw my distress and was gentle with me. His words echoed Sir Ralph Montagu's.

"*All* men sin and fall short, Thomas," he said, stressing the "all". "The King looked for money to fight foreign wars he shouldn't have fought. When Parliament wouldn't agree, he was careless of their rights. He imprisoned and caused to be killed those whom he thought obstructive. He spends money on himself. He intrigues endlessly, and changes his mind more than he changes his hose. He has a particular view of religion which he wishes to impose on all, including the Scots, who will in no wise ever accept it. It involves pretty clothes in church, and incense and fine words, and it may have little to do with Jesus of Nazareth, the carpenter's son. Above all, he believes himself to be on the throne of England by God's express wish. He believes he has a divine right to rule, and so he believes he can do no wrong!"

I was about to object again but he put up his hand to stop me.

"Hear me out, Thomas, because this is very important, and perhaps particularly to you now," he continued. "Don't write me off as Parliament's dupe. Many of us think all this, but still conclude that this imperfect king, for all that he may not be divinely guided, is a better man than his enemies. What study teaches is that everything is uncertain. We have to understand the faults of those we meet, and love them in spite of their imperfections. Sometimes, even *because* of them."

I was curious about what he'd said.

"Why is this so particularly important to me now?" I pressed him.

"Dame Mary's been writing letters," he said, with a half-smile.

"I heard as much from her lips a few weeks since," I said. "She said she would inform the King of what the estate at Grafton has suffered."

"Well, soon you may have the chance to discuss such matters with him directly."

I found it difficult to take in what I thought I'd heard. "Am I to meet the King?" I said, amazed.

"Dame Mary's much moved by what's happened to you," he said quietly. "And Sir Francis was well liked. She also thinks you're a bright spark, a sentiment with which I entirely agree. I wish some of our students here in the college showed as much curiosity and passion."

I blushed. It was a great compliment from a man I already admired.

"Just one thing..." he added.

"What's that, sir?" I asked innocently.

"Keep away from the alehouses while you're here, won't you?" He twinkled again. "Oxford ale rots the brain."

A few days later, on a bright January afternoon, Dame Mary asked me to walk with her in the Physic Garden which lay beside the river opposite the college's gates. As we crossed the road, we nodded to the men who guarded the artillery guns that watched over Oxford, blocking the road. She had me take her by the arm. I was now just a little taller than her.

"It's too bad that there's no time to have you fitted for a new jacket," she said, "but tomorrow you must be brave."

"Why, ma'am?" I said.

"You'll never guess what's to happen to you."

I wasn't going to deny her pleasure. I raised an innocent eyebrow.

"You've an audience with the King, Tom!" There was a note of triumph in her voice.

Even so, as she said the words, I found I was shivering with anticipation.

"I believe it possible you may be able to do something for him. If he likes you."

Now I *was* surprised.

"What ever could I do for him, ma'am? Surely I'm too young to fight in his army?"

Dame Mary pretended to look shocked and then laughed.

"Goodness gracious, no! When I meet your mother in heaven one day, I don't want to tell her I had you enlisted. It's a gentler thing altogether, an appointment of sorts. Be as bright and kind as you can. I always wanted to feel I was able to help you on your way, you know. I owe it to Sarah."

The next day Dame Mary came with me the half mile or so to Christ Church, the college where the King lodged. There was a lot of coming and going through the courtyards, and we were much examined and asked about. Finally a page accompanied us inside and showed us to a handsome carpeted room. I fiddled with a button on my jacket, coughed nervously a great deal, and walked up and down endlessly as we waited, making Dame Mary laugh out loud.

In a little while there was a summons from another solemn courtier. For a second I froze, until Dame Mary smoothed the collar of my jacket and pressed me forward. Feeling more alone than I'd ever done in my life, I followed the courtier through the door into the drawing room that lay beyond. At the far end of the room was a slight figure with a delicately boned face framed by a rather scrappy beard. The hair was long, a distinctive chestnut colour. He turned and smiled at me as I entered. I bowed as low as I knew how, surprised at his lack of height. I had the idea that kings should be large and physically impressive.

He stammered, "N-n-n-no need for that, boy. Stand up, stand up. C-c-c-come over here and look at this." He beckoned me over to the room's far side, where a picture sat balanced against the wall on a table.

"W-w-what do you think?"

I remembered Josiah, who'd so often tried to engage me in discussion about the pictures he loved so dearly. To calm my nerves I tried to imagine I was talking with Josiah and not the King. The painting showed a man on a horse, surveying the land of a great park. It could have been the park at Grafton, and for a brief moment I was overwhelmed by memories of the place I'd loved so much. I swallowed hard, and looked at paint and canvas intently. On closer inspection I decided it really wasn't very good.

"It's very pleasing, Your Majesty," I suggested, lying through my teeth.

"Y-y-yes?"

I wasn't going to get away with that. I could tell he saw straight through me. I should have to speak the truth.

"There's not much life to the horse, is there, Your Majesty? He seems more marble than flesh."

74

The King stepped back, looking at the painting and then back at me. For a moment, I thought I was going to be sent on my way forthwith. Then he broke into loud laughter and spoke again, this time without a trace of a stammer.

"Nor life anywhere else in the painting, I'd say. A great disappointment. And this is an artist they say will go far. I fear he may have to, if he's to make a living. Now what about this?"

And he drew me by the shoulder to one side, where a small tapestry hung from the wall. The colours sang in the dim light. It was a Biblical scene, Lazarus raised from the tomb, and the astonishment and joy written on the faces of the characters portrayed seemed to speak straight out of the wool to us.

"You know whose work this is?" the King asked gently.

I knew. "I believe it's Sir Francis Crane's, Your Majesty," I said.

"Indeed it is," he answered. "A lovely man, Sir Francis. A very good judge of art. And a good judge of people. Now tell me about yourself."

And, sitting down at the table opposite the King, I told my story, what there was to tell, about Grafton, about the siege, and about my mother.

When I'd finished, I could have sworn his eyes were

glistening as if they'd become moistened by tears. But surely that couldn't be so?

He stood up abruptly.

"Do you ride?" he asked.

"Well enough, sir."

"Good, good. And play tennis?"

"No, Your Majesty!" I knew there was a game called by that name, but I hadn't a clue how you played it.

"A pity. It's good sport…"

His words hung in the air. The King seemed to have run out of things to say, or lost the thread of our conversation. And then I realized with astonishment that the King was as nervous of talking with me as I was with him. I had thought a king would always be in control, perfectly poised, but now I understood. He was a man, like any other, for good and ill.

"I'm good with a bow, sir," I volunteered, helping him along.

"Are you so? Ten out of ten on the bullseye at 50 paces?" He smiled.

"Maybe, Your Majesty."

"I should hope so."

There was another pause before he spoke again. This time I waited.

"Y-y-you know I have a son? Also called Charles?"

I nodded.

"There's something I should l-l-like from you." He was stammering again.

"Whatever it is, if it's in my power, Your Majesty, I'd be pleased to do it."

"Will you be a friend to him, Thomas?"

I met the Prince of Wales a week later, in his own rooms at Christ Church. He was very slightly older than me, and taller. The first thing I noticed about him was his extraordinarily dark complexion, which didn't speak of England at all. He looked much more like a Spaniard or someone from North Africa. They say there's all kinds of blood on his mother's side.

Henrietta Maria was in and out of England all the time, a remarkable and independent woman by all accounts, although in Oxford people gossiped about her constantly. A bad influence on the King, they said, with all her Catholic ideas.

The Prince of Wales's character was all in his face. It was soft, and a little melancholy. His lips were inclined to pout, making him look sulky. His eyes were often inclined to wander, avoiding those of his companion. Then in an instant they would light up with a new enthusiasm and devilment.

The first time we met he seemed very bored. Perhaps he suspected that I'd been wheeled in to "do him good", in much the same way as his various governors had been. The latest, recently appointed, was the Earl of Berkshire, a fussy and rather irritable man of about 40, who'd looked me over briefly the same day I'd met the King, checking my suitability. From the way he ran his eye over my jacket and breeches, he didn't think much of my tailoring, but clearly he hadn't been able to find any other fault glaring enough to reject me.

From the first, the Prince of Wales was very anxious to tell me about himself and his exploits. He didn't seem curious about *me* in the least.

On the floor of the room in Christ Church there was an array of chess pieces, bits of card, clay figures and pottery. The Prince was playing war games. The clutter represented the dispositions of the various forces, and now he had a captive audience to whom he could explain it.

"Edgehill," he said carelessly. "The Battle of Edgehill. You know what happened, of course?"

Even if I'd known, politeness and the way he spoke to me would have demanded the answer "no". I knew only that it had been the first engagement between the King's army and Parliament eighteen months ago, and that things had gone better for the King at Edgehill than at any time since.

"I was in the thick of it," he boasted.

I tried to be enthusiastic. "Were you?" I asked.

"Damn near killed, I shouldn't wonder. My regiment was in the front line, you know."

I paid homage to his bravery.

"Of course, they wouldn't let me lead the charge. Too bad for morale if I'd been wounded." He began to move the chess pieces around.

"We were *here*. And then we got separated from the men, *here*, on the dip slope from the ridge. It was all that idiot Hyde's fault."

I nodded sagely, though I didn't have a clue who Hyde was.

"What happened?" I asked, not knowing if the answer I'd get would be fact or fiction.

"It was a real scrap. I saw hundreds killed. Blood everywhere, and hacked-off limbs thick on the ground."

"Goodness," I said.

He narrowed his eyes at me, perhaps wondering at the sincerity of my interest. "Hyde and Hinton tried to persuade me to retreat," he went on, "but I pulled out my pistol and told them not to be such cowards."

(Later, I asked Richard Hardisty if he knew whether this was true. "That's not *quite* what I heard," said

Richard. "Actually Hyde and Hinton probably saved his life. They shot a soldier who saw a chance of glory in capturing the Prince of Wales for parade in London. They were only there because of the little fool's insistence at getting too close to the action!")

I let the Prince exercise himself for a full half-hour or more telling me about his incredible exploits, until finally he changed the subject abruptly and commanded, "Do you play chess?"

I said I did, and he swept up the pieces on to a finely made board. Each square had been perfectly cut and lacquered. Ivory was inlaid around the edges.

"Chess is a battle game, too," he said. "I bet I'll beat you."

He played very badly. Try as I might, I couldn't find a way to let him win.

"Beginner's luck," he said crossly, after the second checkmate, and turned away to stare out of the window at the greyness of the courtyard. It seemed he'd had enough of me for the afternoon.

"Would you like me to come and visit you again?" I tried nervously.

He shrugged his shoulders. "As you wish," he said.

Annoyed, I thought to myself, "But you're the future king. It's what you want that counts."

I assumed another summons to see the Prince would be sent to Dame Mary's rooms in due course, but after a week there was no news. I felt bad. I'd been given a simple task by the King, and somehow I'd managed to let him down. The Prince had obviously taken a dislike to me. My services were no longer required. It was a very wet Easter, and I moped around the college rooms at Magdalen. What had I done wrong?

Richard Hardisty came across me in the library trying to cheer myself up by reading Homer's story of the wanderings of Odysseus. I told him what was worrying me.

"I'll see what I can find out," he said. "But don't make too much of it. These people live life on a whim. You're learning what it's like to be royal."

Later that day he sought me out.

"No need to worry," he said. "The Prince has the measles. In fact, he's quite unwell. His life's not in danger, the doctors say, but there's been a fever and now he's very weak. Leave it a while. They'll send for you. Have you ever had it?"

"I think so," I said, "when I was very little. At least, that's what my mother once told me. I don't remember."

They called me a fortnight later, as the daffodils were making Oxford look a bit brighter after the mud and wet of winter and the days grew longer. The Prince was lying on a couch. He was a bad colour, his swarthy skin blotched and pallid. The eyes were dull, but he managed a weak smile as I entered.

"I hope you don't catch it," he said. "I don't recommend it as a way of spending time." His first words were more friendly than anything he'd said on the previous visit.

I read to him for an hour or so about Sir Francis Drake's bravery in the wars with Spain. He fell asleep once, and jokingly complained that the stories made him feel seasick.

"Come again on Friday," he said. "I'll feel stronger then. And bring with you a book that doesn't tell of so many waves and drownings!"

Three days later he was still poorly, and he continued to be so for some weeks. Gradually, however, he began to feel better, and as his health improved, so did our friendship. We enjoyed the spring sunshine, riding out into the countryside around Oxford.

The Prince was a creature of terrible moods. Some days he was silent and withdrawn for long periods of time. Then suddenly a madcap idea would occur to him, and I'd have to go along with it, trying to block anything I thought would end in tears. It could be anything from chasing some poor yeoman's sheep (in the Prince's head they'd become Roundheads) to announcing to some unsuspecting girl he wished to make her the future Queen of England. Pretty girls often seemed to play a part in his plans. From a distance the Earl of Berkshire looked on disapprovingly. Apart from me, he was the only person who ever seemed to say no to the Prince.

With John Poynter, it had always been me who egged him on. Now the boot was on the other foot. I was the goody-goody being tempted into bad behaviour by someone else. But it *was* fun, no doubt about it!

In helping the Prince to recover from his illness, I'd slowly begun to get better myself. Looking after someone else had taken my mind off my own misfortune. I realized it had been six months since the sack of Grafton. How distant it now seemed, and how my life had changed as a result! If I thought about it, I felt guilty to know I no longer wore my grief for a lost mother like a weight around my neck. In a strange way, the dreadful events at Grafton had been the making of me.

The days I spent in the company of the Prince of Wales were a heady time of naughtiness and freedom. I continued to live at Magdalen, but the Prince and I spent every day at large in Oxford. If he'd been a lesser person, we'd have been in the stocks more than once for our pains. As it was, the court just had to put up with us, though with a frowning face.

Once the Earl of Berkshire went so far as to cuff my royal companion around the ear for unseemly laughter in church, but that was as far as any punishment went. We peeped through the keyholes of bedrooms belonging to young women of the court in the hope of catching them undressing. We booby-trapped doors so that buckets fell on elderly courtiers. We rode our horses through puddles so that smartly dressed citizens of Oxford were spattered with mud. I'm ashamed to recall our dreadful behaviour. Put it down to the devil finding work for idle hands to do. But what more terrible things would the heir to the throne have done, if I hadn't been there to stop him? How many times did I say, "Charlie, you just can't do that!"

To which he would always reply scornfully, "Odds fish, Tom, don't you know the meaning of fun?"

Then one day I found him unusually gloomy in his rooms.

"My father's decided to put me to work," he groaned. "Now you'll have your way. The fun's about to stop for good!"

"I can't believe that," I said, trying to cheer him up.

"It's true," he said. "The Scots are marching south. The King says I must grow up. It's all hands on deck."

"About time too!" said Richard Hardisty later when I told him about the conversation. "There are things he can do to help. Time he earned his keep!"

"The King's asked to see me, too," I said. Richard pulled a face, as if to say, "Lucky you!"

"What do you think he wants?" I asked.

Richard shrugged. "Who knows? I should wish for something easier than wet-nursing a prince, if I were you!"

✕ ✕ ✕

I'd encountered the King just once or twice since that first interview with him, and was nervous to be in his presence again. To be honest, I was afraid to be told off. What I actually got was his sincere thanks.

"It c-c-can't have been easy for you," he said.

I was about to make excuses but he waved them away.

"N-n-n-no! Don't tell me anything I don't want to kn-n-now," he added. "I understand my son very well. But now the Prince of Wales must start to take his responsibilities more seriously. The people expect to see him." He fidgeted with his cane. "I c-c-can't be everywhere, and sometimes in my absence the commanders take too much upon themselves. If Ch-ch-ch..." Sometimes he had to stop in the middle of a sentence and then start again, because of his stammer. "If Charlie's in the room, they have to behave themselves. D'you see?"

I made noises of understanding.

"You've proved yourself very capable," he continued. "Dame M-m-Mary always told me you would! How *is* she, by the way?"

I told him she was beginning to suffer from gout, and that getting about Oxford was becoming harder. He nodded sympathetically, but I don't know that he'd heard what I'd said.

"I shall be t-t-travelling more often again shortly," he said. "F-f-for one thing, enemies are gathering around Oxford, like so many dogs around the fox. I'd like you to come with me. We need young people about us. If there are too many greybeards, the court's too stodgy and stale. What do you think?"

I could hardly refuse, could I?

I told Dame Mary at dinner that night. "May I go?" I asked.

"You don't have to ask!" she said at once. "Of course you must. It's what I always hoped for. You'll be a great man one day, Tom. You must take your chances as they come!"

"Do you know what he has in mind for you?" asked Richard Hardisty, picking bread from a bowl on the long wooden table and dipping it in his thin and watery soup.

It was becoming difficult for supplies to reach Oxford from the West, and food was in shorter measure than it had been all spring.

"His Majesty wishes to take some paintings with him on campaign. He wants me to look after them."

Pushing away his bowl in disgust, Richard snorted. "So it's true?"

I was surprised by the tone of his voice. In the heat of the moment I felt he was belittling my commission, and slighting the King. There was part of me that badly wanted to pick up arms to fight for the royal cause, though I had no training and wouldn't have lasted two minutes on the battlefield. That same part of me knew there was something second best about looking after a few pieces from the royal art collection. Richard quickly saw that he'd touched a raw nerve and that I was hurt.

"I'm sorry, Tom," he said. "I didn't mean to offend you. We all know the King loves his pictures, and I'd heard rumours that he always likes to keep his favourite things at his side. But, you must admit, it's pretty extraordinary. Which is more important, when England's at war with herself? To be able to look at your choicest trinket from time to time, or to fight effectively? What's wrong with the man?"

Dame Mary was more severe with Richard than I'd ever seen her. "If more people cared about art, there'd be fewer wars," she said sharply. "Don't listen to him, Tom. We're in danger of forgetting what's important in life."

$$\times \times \times$$

I had no idea of what a king's army in progress around the realm was like. After I'd bade a final farewell to

Dame Mary and John Poynter, I suddenly discovered I was part of a mighty procession of humans and machines. In the rear was a baggage train almost the size of an army itself, and somewhere to the back of the procession was the wagon which carried me and my precious cargo.

After the cosiness and fun of Oxford, life on the road was a sobering jump into a river of cold water. After the gentility of Dame Mary's company, I found myself swept along on a torrent of bad language, and caught up in whirlpools of intrigue and rumour.

My master was Sir James Elliman. A groom of the bedchamber, a man trusted by the King for his good advice and ability to make things happen on time and in the right way: I quickly found Sir James to be smooth even when the going was at its roughest. He never made a decision on the spur of the moment. Never once did I hear him raise his voice.

"Do the simple things well," he said quietly to me the first time we met, "and I shall be perfectly content. Do not gamble or drink more than you should. Be at your post when you're required to be. Look after your companions, as you'd hope to be looked after. Do you understand me?"

Mind you, it took time to earn his respect. At first I

think he was suspicious, perhaps even annoyed, at having a mere boy foisted on him. He assumed I and my pictures were yet another royal whim that had to be tolerated, as if life wasn't difficult enough already. Then, as he began to see I could take care of myself, could ride well and knew how to speak to people, he took me into his confidence and began to use me to carry messages.

Apart from Sir James, the junior pages and courtiers became my friends, particularly Alexander Fitzsimmons. Alex was well-born and could be a dreadful snob, though at his best he was clever and amusing company. As a rider he was completely fearless, and would encourage his horse to take in its stride obstacles I thought completely impossible.

"Come *on*," he'd shout behind him as he disappeared over some hedge or gate. "What keeps you?"

Alex and I talked endlessly about our fellow-companions, speculating about what might befall us, and trying to read the mind of the King. It wasn't always easy. Before we even set off on our travels, when it seemed he might have to fight for his life the very next day, he went hunting at Woodstock.

When this became known I said, "Well things can't

be *so* bad, can they? Not if the King has the time for shooting deer!"

Alexander, who liked to play the man of the world, said airily, "I don't know so much. I've heard it's what he always does in a crisis."

Until we reached Cornwall in mid-summer, we saw little action, and were never in danger. By then we'd been to Worcester and back, fought a battle at Cropredy near Banbury (though I never saw a shot fired), toasted the birth of a new daughter to the King, and heard the dreadful news that the King's forces under Prince Rupert in Yorkshire had been routed at Marston Moor. York was taken by Parliament too, and the shame was enough that Lord Newcastle took himself abroad in exile.

Yet the King was cheerful throughout. I encountered him from time to time as he settled himself in some great house or another, and as I decorated his chambers with the scenes and portraits he loved best. There were maybe twenty pictures in my safe keeping, commissioned from Europe's finest painters, men like Rubens and Van Dyck. We had a cart for their transport and a driver, Edward, who grumbled his way from place to place. After the disaster at York, I offered my concern to the King one day.

"It'll all be for the best, Thomas," he said cheerfully. "God will look after us. The cause is just, and our enemies misguided. We must have faith."

I found that for once I couldn't share his complete confidence.

"Don't you ever doubt, Your Majesty?" I dared to say.

He looked at me very straightforwardly. "Of course I *doubt*, Tom. Sometimes I think I shall be imprisoned and the key thrown away. But we have to *work* at faith. It's no easy work."

It was common gossip in the camp that the losses to our side in Yorkshire had been terrible. It was rumoured that thousands had been killed by pike-thrusts and musket bullets.

It was only when we were in Cornwall that I saw the scale of what war could do. We came across part of Parliament's defeated army after a battle at Lostwithiel, a column of maybe 400 bedraggled and wounded men. Their clothes were in rags, and their limbs much the same. I saw with horror that some arms and legs were mere rotting stumps. I turned away my gaze from men whose eyes had been put out. All were without food and hope. There was nothing we could do. We lacked medicines and food to make them well again. We drove on, and left them to their fate.

We had our own little drama along the road. The Cornish countryside was bleak and unforgiving, even in late summer and autumn. There were many places where an army could be caught unawares and ambushed. Our line of wagons had begun to straggle and lengthen in wild weather. My head was down as I rode into the teeth of a gale beside Edward, and I struggled to understand the meaning of the sudden shouts of anxiety from in front of us. I looked up and saw horses rearing and turning. Then I heard a volley of shots ring out, though I could not see who fired them for the smoke that suddenly hung over the road. At last, and nearly too late, I obeyed a harshly issued instruction to dismount and take shelter behind the wagons if I valued my life. I felt rather than heard the musket fire that might have been the end of me, as it ripped the air apart and shredded the canvas behind my head.

I brought my horse into the lee of the cart, and dived for the cover its broad solid shape afforded. Edward was there too. For some minutes all was confusion. We were supposed always to be under the protection of a few foot soldiers, and from behind the wagon I could see them desperately struggling hand to hand with strangers whose faces were smeared with dung and dirt. I saw Adam Jobling, a man I'd come to know well and liked much for his cheerful humour, tussle with one of the enemy who towered head and shoulders above him. The roaring giant pinned Adam's sword arm with his own, and then brought through a treacherous left fist to bury a knife deep in Adam's stomach. My friend was hurled back by the violence of the blow. He convulsed, and fell stone dead before our eyes.

It seemed like hours, but can have been only minutes before reinforcements arrived on horseback from up the line. Seeing they were outnumbered, our ambushers retreated into the safety of the dark countryside. After the noise of battle, all was suddenly and eerily quiet.

The next morning we had the solemn duty of burying five of our company. Had it not been for their bravery and willingness to die, many more of us might not have survived the attack. They had held the line just long enough.

$$\times \bigtimes \times$$

In November 1644 we returned to Oxford for the winter, and I think Dame Mary found me rather changed.

"I can't believe how you've grown," she said when she first greeted me. "Now I really do have to look up to you."

I could very nearly match Richard Hardisty inch for inch.

"How hangs the King's gallery?" he asked with a half-smile.

"As straight as he'd want, Richard," I said.

"You didn't lose anything on the way, then?"

"We came close once near Liskeard, surprised by one or two Roundheads who'd lost their way," I replied, adapting the truth for Dame Mary's benefit. "But our guards beat off the ruffians easily enough."

Dame Mary seemed to turn a little pale at even this much. Richard laughed, "Well at least you have no war wounds to show us."

"Hush, Richard," said Dame Mary, "I have bad dreams about such matters, as it is."

The winter passed uneasily. Archbishop Laud, the King's friend, was executed for treason. The King was visited by commissioners from Parliament to persuade him he should make peace on their terms. They were sent back to London with a flea in their ear.

Richard Hardisty shook his head. "He should find a compromise," he said. "Really he should! These men have money. They have power, except that the King won't listen to their advice. That's all they want, when it comes down to it. If you've worked all your life for country and family, if you've built yourself a business empire, you're bound to want a share of power. We're past the time when a King can say "jump" and you jump, whoever you are. Who does he think he is – King Henry VIII? Next he'll be taking a brace of new wives to himself. One day you may have influence, Thomas. Use it well, won't you? Make him see sense."

As the days lengthened, it was clear that another summer would be spent fighting. In the May of 1645 the King held a Council of War at Stow, 40 miles to the west of Oxford.

Now Parliament had leaders to match the King for

strength of character. Though Thomas Fairfax was their general, all the talk was of Cromwell from Huntingdon. I remembered Alice Montagu mentioning him years before as an important person her father knew. But only now had he developed a fearsome reputation as a man of iron will. Where once there'd been militias and soldiery in different parts of England, each fighting their own individual battles with the King, now we faced a single force united under Fairfax and Cromwell. They called themselves the New Model Army. Alexander scoffed at them.

"What's this new model, but the same men as before, in different clothes, no better or worse?" he mocked one day.

"They say there's a renewed determination among them to see the King humbled," I replied.

"Remember your Bible, Tom. 'He hath brought down the mighty from their seat!' "

Alexander was very inclined to quote from the Bible, and not always entirely seriously. I didn't like the habit, and I could have pointed out that what he said might equally have applied to the King.

We agreed that Leicester was an attractive target for the King and his generals. It wasn't too far from Oxford, its garrison was thin and could never defend the three miles of earthworks and walls which circled the city.

"He needs a victory," said Alexander sagely. "The loss at Marston Moor must be avenged. Leicester's the place!"

✕✕✕

So, at the end of May, the uneasy peace of winter was left behind and we marched through Ashby de la Zouch and Loughborough in high spirits. By 28th May our horses were outside Leicester, and by the 30th the city was surrounded. This time the baggage train was close to the action – the King was confident of success. We would see, hear, taste the battle. It was a moment of high excitement for Alexander and me.

Not so for our driver, Edward. He spat on the ground when he heard the news. "I would we were a few miles in the rear. I would so," he muttered.

On the afternoon of the 30th the artillery trained their guns on the Newarke, where the walls were weakest, and in just three hours the cannon balls had smashed their way through. At a safe distance from musket fire, Alexander and I watched awestruck at what gunpowder can achieve. Its acrid smell was heavy on the smoky air which hung over collapsed piles of masonry. They were all that remained of defences which had stood firm for hundreds of years.

Then, at midnight, a co-ordinated infantry attack caught the town by surprise and Leicester's defences were breached in four other places. Our soldiers were in no mood to show mercy as they pressed home the advantage. They went in with grim faces and flashing blades. It was commonly believed that Leicester citizens sympathetic to the crown had been lynched by the townspeople. Throughout recent years the town had developed a reputation as being rather too helpful to Parliament's cause, and now it was due for punishment.

At four the next afternoon, Sir James told me to take a message to the Guildhall in the town centre. Alexander was bidden to ride with me. What we saw was deeply shocking.

There were bodies lying in the streets, not just men, but women and children too. The afternoon sun was stiflingly hot and already the stench of death hung in the still air. The hooded crows scattered as we rode by but then settled a few yards away, eyeing up a possible meal. We passed a doorstep where a young woman lay in a pool of blood, her mouth gaping open in a death scream. I glanced across at Alexander. He was pale in the strong sunlight, his face stretched and tense.

"Are you all right?" I asked.

"Yes," he choked. "Just keep riding."

When we'd delivered the message safely and returned to camp, Alexander wandered off by himself. I found him washing his face at a stream. He'd been sick.

"How can that have happened?" I asked, dazed. The smell of putrefying bodies hung in my nostrils, in my clothes.

He shook his head.

"Those children can't have been any threat to armed soldiers," I pressed. He rounded on me.

"What do you know? You weren't there, were you? There must have been a reason. There must!"

But in our hearts we both knew crimes had been committed that day. Innocents had been killed. Surely, I thought, there'll be revenge for what happened at Leicester, either from God or the laws of natural justice? You get back what you put in, my mother used to say. You reap what you sow, king or commoner alike.

A fortnight after the siege of Leicester I found myself in the lush Northampton countryside once again. The King's army was camped near Clipston just outside Market Harborough, and close to the village of Naseby.

In recent days, our scouts had been constantly reporting that the King's army was being tracked mile for mile by Sir Thomas Fairfax. At the beginning of May, Cromwell and Fairfax had set out to lay siege to Oxford, and had we not been on the move ourselves against Leicester, Magdalen College and all the other great buildings of Oxford I'd grown to love so well might have been razed to the ground. As it was we forced the Roundheads to divert their attention elsewhere, so at least some good came from the dreadful business.

Now, though, the enemy was watching and waiting, looking for a moment to inflict the maximum damage. But the people who counted, up to and including the King, didn't want to know.

On the eve of the battle which was to take place at Naseby, the King spent a complete day hunting, this time at Fawsley Park near Daventry, miles away from his expectant army.

"It's only his way of preparing for battle," mused Alexander. "He's sharpening his sword."

"It could look like foolishness," I said crossly.

On his return the King was immediately faced with the truth. Word came from up the road that the Roundheads had picked off some of our rearguard. They'd been supposed to be on the lookout for enemy activity, and *still* they'd been overrun.

The commanders held an emergency council of war, while the rest of us waited anxiously in our tents and carts, cooking and singing songs to keep up our spirits. We knew a major battle was to come. And it was no secret that we might be outnumbered, by as much as two to one.

Once it had been decided that we'd stand and fight, even though it was late in the evening, the King went on his rounds encouraging the men. There was a light in his eyes.

"H-h-how are you, boys?" he said quietly. Even at this moment he had time for us.

"Fine, Your Majesty," said Alexander who was feeling more cheerful than I was. I stood beside him shivering with cold and fear.

"The outcome isn't in doubt, you know," the King said, looking at me, and laughing. "You needn't be a *doubting* Thomas! Fairfax's men are a rabble. They'll be no match for proper soldiers with right on their side."

He was in that mood of complete certainty which made disagreement impossible. I couldn't look him in the eye. Alexander saved the day.

"May tomorrow be the day England understands who should best rule it, sir," he said without blinking.

"We must pray so," the King agreed. He looked at me keenly. "Be strong, Thomas! What are we carrying with us on this trip?" He meant the paintings.

I told him.

"May I see the Van Dyck?" he asked. There was a portrait of the King, by the Dutch master, a very good likeness, I thought. I unwrapped it partially from its covering, and turned it so that the light from the fire fell on it. The colours glowed, and the King's noble face shone out into the night.

"I wish I felt now as blithe and bonny as I looked then," he said jokingly. He was looking for a compliment.

"You look every inch as a king should, Your Majesty," I said gamely.

And with our flattery ringing in his ears he left to continue his rounds.

The preparations for battle began next morning at first light. The fighting men, both foot soldiers and cavalry, moved up from the ridge where we were camped to forward positions at Dust Hill. A strange and ominous atmosphere hung over the baggage train like morning mist.

"Shall we see how close we can get to the battle?" asked Alexander at about seven o'clock. "God's truth, this waiting is too much to bear!"

We told Edward what we were doing, and asked him if he'd cover for us if anyone wanted to know where we were.

"You wish to get me into trouble, is that it?" he moaned. "When you've seen as much as I, you'll be glad to be as far from guns and pikes as possible. But boys must learn to be men, I suppose. Go on, be off with you!"

Privately, I agreed with Edward that leaving our stations was a bad idea, but I didn't think Alexander should go alone.

We saddled our horses and picked a way around Clipston village to a hedge backed by a dense wood, following the general direction we knew the battlefield to lie, and using our ears for sounds of any engagement. We reckoned we were safe. No army could penetrate the thicket behind us.

Before us, the ground dropped away and there was a clear view to the open plain between two low ridges, one of which was occupied by our men, far to the right. The ridge furthest away and to our left, maybe a mile and a half distant, seemed empty at first, until our eyes picked out occasional movement behind the trees and bushes that dotted the skyline. Enemy scouts, we guessed. Nearer to us, the hedges on either side of our troops created a funnel which broadened out on to the plain. The King's army looked magnificent, sun glinting on metal, the cavalry with their horses under perfect control, the foot soldiers in solid blocks of uncompromising steel. How could anyone stop such a mighty force?

"Where are the Roundheads?" Alexander breathed.

"Thought better of it, perhaps?"

"More likely beyond the hill, biding their time."

"They may think to take us by surprise."

We didn't have long to wait. With the sun climbing higher in the sky, the brow of the ridge began to grow bristles and then a beard as Fairfax's men and horses moved out of cover and began to swarm down the hill towards the King's armies. As they did so our cavalry on the right wing spurred their horses to meet the enemy at full charge. As they moved out of the funnel of hedges on to the plain, the numbers of our men seemed to swell by the second.

"It's Prince Rupert," shouted Alex, recognizing the standard that led the charge. "Look at them go!"

In a matter of seconds, the armies were entangled, man on man, in a frenzy of hacking and thrusting. We saw soldiers knocked over like tiny ninepins and crushed under the feet of other men or horses, and heard the coarse, obscene roar of battle as the armies clashed. It was dreadful to watch, but we could not draw our eyes away. In only a few minutes the ground was strewn with the dead and dying of both sides. As they moved forward, men fell over the corpses in front of them.

On the far side, the King's cavalry drove clean through to the rear of the enemy. The Roundheads began to turn and run as Prince Rupert pressed the charge on and on, towards the ring of Parliamentary musketeers defending wagons high on the ridge.

Meanwhile, in the centre of the field, the fighting was more cautious. Neither of the two armies seemed anxious to grasp the nettle since the defences of both sides were so well constructed. Walls of pikes had been thrown up, angled out to face the opposition, shielding the men behind them and preventing any advance from the cavalry. From time to time, small bands of soldiers skirmished half-heartedly, each attempting to draw the other into an attack through the middle which might expose their rear.

"Is that not the King?" asked Alex, pointing to the right.

"Where?" I said, shielding my eyes from the sun.

"See! There, with the reserve, back up the hill, waiting his time," replied Alex excitedly.

"I hope he does not wait too long," I said.

For on the side nearest us, it was the King's men who were now in disarray and under pressure from the enemy's cavalry.

"Why can't our men hold steady?" asked Alex in dismay.

"We're too few," I said, teeth gritted, beginning to doubt success. In front of us our cavalry were trying to straighten their lines and regroup, but the weight of the enemy's numbers meant we were losing ground by the minute. I watched one officer of the King turn his horse half a dozen times in an attempt to find space to run back at the enemy, but with each turn he found them pressing hard in on him again. Finally, his horse reared on end, and I lost sight of him as he collapsed into a mêlée of men.

In the centre now, too, as the battle grew more intense, there were the first signs that our shape couldn't hold. As the infantry of the two armies finally came together with a chorus of shouting and dreadful curses our men were forced backwards under the onslaught of the enemy pikes. There was no flinching from the fight, but again we were outnumbered, and in danger of being overwhelmed. Men slipped and stumbled in desperate hand-to-hand fighting. We saw a number fall who would never rise to their feet again.

Now the King moved decisively forward. We could see the royal standard move into the killing ground. For a few minutes everything went well. The addition of his force to the line took the momentum of the battle towards the Parliamentary rear. For a moment it seemed as if we might be about to win the day, in spite of inferior numbers. Then there was a sudden check in the advance.

"Move on, move on!" shouted Alex in frustration, as if they might hear his advice. "To the left of you, now!"

For at that moment, disaster befell us. When it seemed that if the King were to pursue his advance with vigour the Parliamentary infantry would be vanquished, he suddenly stopped and turned his horse to the right, as if to consult with one of the commanders who rode beside him. Without thinking, those behind followed his example. In that little moment, the enemy had the opportunity to reassemble and redouble their attack, against a force that was now stationary.

In just a few minutes more, a full-scale rout of our forces was under way, and proud soldiers of the King were turning tail and running. We saw at least one set of colours fall, snatched away in triumph by the King's enemies. Men were being taken prisoner, and others slaughtered where they stood.

"What shall we do?" I asked hopelessly.

"Let's go to the baggage, Tom, or the Roundheads may be there before us."

We retraced our steps at a gallop, and in a quarter-hour were back at the camp.

Edward was pacing up and down anxiously, studying his feet. He shook his fist at us for being away so long, and was relieved and then cast down again all at once, as we told him what we'd seen.

"Everything may be lost, Edward," I blurted out. "What should we do? Where's Sir James?"

"How would I know?" he said, gesturing at the collection of carts and covered wagons that surrounded us. People were wandering aimlessly, waiting, sheltering from the heat of the sun.

"There's nothing we can do," he muttered. "Not until there's orders. And those who could give the orders have other things on their minds. If what you say's right."

He went back to his pacing, hands behind his back, looking greyer and more stooped by the minute.

Soon the battle-weary soldiers began to arrive at the camp. None of those who'd been in the thick of the fight had anything encouraging to report. One or two high-ranking officers, badly wounded by musket, sword or pike, rode into the camp as best they could, hanging off their startled horses. They were looking for safety and the binding of their wounds, but there was little that could be done for them. Many a time I'd heard soldiers say how a shattered leg goes to gangrene quickly in summer heat. Better to take a head wound and die at once, they used to mutter. Seeing the state of these men as they returned, panic began to set in among the camp.

I didn't see Sir James arrive, but suddenly he was beside me, as apparently unruffled as ever, even though he too was covered in grime. There were streaks of blood on his face and forearm. His sleeves were torn. He drew me to one side, away from Edward.

"I don't know how this may go," he said quietly. "At

sea, when a ship goes down, there's sometimes an instruction that every man should look out for himself. If it were to come to a choice between His Majesty's paintings and you Tom, you should save yourself. Understood?"

"I would never desert my post, sir," I said in an agony of guilt and hopelessness.

"You're a boy, Tom. And you shouldn't be here. Hear what I say!"

"Yes, sir," I croaked. I could see now there was an open wound on his arm. "Are you hurt, Sir James?"

He glanced at his arm as if he hadn't noticed anything wrong until that very moment.

"Nothing but a scratch," he replied carelessly. It was very much more than that.

Under Sir James's supervision, the baggage train was set on another of its many journeys. We were to make for Leicester with as much speed as we could. Alex sat with me inside the awning on the cart, beside its precious and ridiculous cargo, away from the sun, our legs dangling from the back over the road.

The road away from Naseby was complete mayhem. We travelled slowly because of the size of the cart and Edward's careful driving, overtaken by panicking soldiers on foot and horseback as well as other carts and wagons. The hard surface was rutted and the ride was bumpy and uncomfortable. As we turned a sharp corner, we came across what at first sight seemed to be an accident. One cart was in the ditch and another on its side. We stopped, and over my shoulder I saw Edward confronting two men. Their tone was harsh, their manner threatening. They were Roundheads. They had to be. Neither Alexander nor I could hear what was said on either side. We only saw the stunning blow that felled poor Edward to the ground. As the two of us jumped from our perches we found ourselves overpowered by yet more soldiers who came at us from the bushes beside the road.

"Whoa, not so fast," said a crude, cackling voice. "I swear the King's soldiers get younger by the turn. Here's some not long from their mothers' breasts."

Alex was always stronger than his size at first suggested. He twisted and turned, snapping out of the arms of the ruffian who held him. I saw Alexander's hand slip the knife from his belt, and plunge it into his assailant's side.

The Roundhead was wounded but not fatally, and his sword arm was still free.

"No, Alex," I screamed, struggling desperately to loose myself. It was too late. Before I pitched forward into unconsciousness from the blow that fell on my skull, I remember seeing the Roundhead's sword scythe viciously towards Alex's chest.

When I came round, it took me some time to grasp what was happening. A familiar voice called me by name, and told me to drink water from the flask that was being offered, yet at first I couldn't identify who talked to me.

I felt sick, and had vomited twice before I understood that the voice I knew belonged to Ralph Montagu, Alice's father. It seemed incredible, but it was so.

I was propped under a tree at the side of the road and facing away from it. Sir Ralph was throwing water on my face, urgently trying to focus my attention, speaking in a fierce whisper.

"Listen, Thomas," he hissed. "You must listen to me. You've but one chance and you must take it. No quarter's being given. Nothing awaits you here other than murder, and even I may not be able to give you safe passage. Find your way to Ashton. You'll be received there, trust me.

"But I'm the King's servant," I said weakly, almost delirious from the wound on my head.

"The King's as good as finished after today. We've ransacked his wagons. There may be evidence of treason, of collusion with the French and goodness knows what else. His army's suffered huge losses. They say there are thousands of dead back there. You must go."

"Where's Alex?" I asked, suddenly anxious for my friend as my head slowly cleared. "Where is he?"

"Your friend's dead, Tom. I was too late to save him…" Sir Ralph's voice was becoming ever more urgent.

I clapped my hands to my head as if to stop myself hearing the awful news.

"…but I'm not too late to save you. If you'll just gather yourself up and go."

"How?"

"Think, Thomas. Northampton is twelve miles away to the south, and Ashton a handful more. You could be there by early tomorrow."

With an aching head and a reluctant and heavy heart, I accepted Sir Ralph's offer, and, slowly stumbling by a woodland path, took myself on a wide arc around the battlefield and off to the south, to the safety of Ashton. I never expected to reach there unscathed. Only luck and Sir Ralph's fortunate intervention preserved me. Edward, Alexander, Sir James: they had all perished that day. Once again I had been spared while those I loved died at the hands of strangers.

July 1645 – August 1647

For months after Naseby I stayed with the Montagus at Ashton, closed in on myself and sad. As I thought about the horrors I'd seen I mourned for my mother all over again, as well as Alexander and those others who had given their lives. Had the cause been worth it? Sir Ralph would not have said so. Richard Hardisty would have doubted it. And these were the men I respected most in the world.

I often went to Grafton. The Roundheads had pulled down the remains of the lovely house. Some of the stone had been carried off, and some lay strewn about the gardens. People I'd known would occasionally come and greet me, but I had no heart for them.

I moped for Peter Aston and Josiah Bewley too, both casualties of the war. Josiah had lasted only a few pitiful weeks after the siege. His will had been broken. With Grafton's downfall, he had nothing to live for. Peter Aston had taken ill not long afterwards. Weakened by his ill-treatment and lack of good food, he'd finally died of pneumonia in the April just past. I sat and watched the larks rising on the breeze, their sound filling the sky. They were a sign of hope, but for a while nothing could touch me, or brighten my mood.

Only Alice's energy and understanding kept me from giving up. She knew when to argue, and when to let me be. As a child she'd always been noisy. Now, she'd learned how to be gentle too, when she needed.

In time Sir Ralph returned from fighting for good, though for a year or so he was only an occasional visitor to Ashton. Through him I learned that the King had been betrayed by the Scots he'd thought to befriend since the French wouldn't help him. Instead of making an alliance with Charles against the English Parliament, the Scots imprisoned him and finally handed him over when they thought it was most to their advantage. What a strange thought: the King a prisoner in his own land!

Once I would have thought it impossibly wrong, back in the days when I worshipped the ground on which Charles stood. Now, like many others, I wondered whether he'd partly brought this fate upon himself. Why couldn't he have listened to wise counsel a little more? It had been common knowledge that even in the heat of battle he would overrule his commanders' opinion, for no reason that could be fathomed. Yet, mixed with these feelings was my guilt. Like so many others, I had left him in his hour of need.

Gradually, almost without noticing it was happening, I took over as steward for the Ashton estate. The old man who'd been in charge for years died, and there wasn't anyone obvious for the job. I'd been helping out, and slowly more and more was put on my shoulders. I didn't mind. The busier I was, the more cheerful I became and the less time I had to think.

Then one day in February of 1647, news came that caught me off-balance. Alice announced it at dinner.

"The King's come again to Northamptonshire," she said, teasingly.

"How do you know?" I asked. I spite of myself, her words made my heart beat faster.

"My friend, Abigail Wheatman, had it from someone who was in Northampton today. It was on everyone's lips at All Saints Church, she says."

"So of course it's true," I said mockingly.

"It is," she said defiantly, holding her ground. "Though it's of no concern to me. I was never his supporter. I thought you'd be more interested…"

"Where do the Northampton gossips say he is then?"

I said after a pause, trying not to show that actually, yes, I was fascinated.

"You see!" Alice triumphed. "You do want to know. Any little thing about him, and you're hooked. If he snapped his fingers, you'd go running, even now."

If we'd been by ourselves, we'd have quarrelled, as we sometimes did. Sir Ralph and Lady Montagu were present, and her sister too, so I kept quiet. Alice wouldn't let it go.

"It's somewhere not so far away..." she teased.

I refused to rise to the bait.

"Go on, have a guess," she said.

Sir Ralph lost patience. "Don't be silly, Alice! Holdenby, Tom. The King's at Holdenby, under some kind of house arrest. He's been there all this last week."

Alice looked deflated, and rather cross with her father for spoiling the fun. She knew me better than I knew myself. As far as the King was concerned, I'd always been like a moth with a candle flame. I was drawn. Despite all that had happened I still felt sorry for him. The slightness of his stature, the delicacy of his features and tastes made him seem vulnerable. I didn't know the wicked tyrant others claimed to see.

Holdenby House was a fine place to be under arrest, if you had to be arrested. The King's wife,

Henrietta Maria, owned it in name, though by now she was far away in France. Holdenby was a magnificent residence, well situated eight miles to the north of Northampton, light and airy, grander almost than any other house in the land, a palace of glass. Around it the country was all hills and dales, dotted with sheep. When I was small, I'd been taken to admire this magnificent site. It was celebrated as a local wonder.

Over the course of a few days an idea began to form. Finally, I plucked up the courage to voice it to Sir Ralph.

"I'd like to write to the King, sir," I said.

"Why not?" he replied. I was surprised: I thought he'd be against the notion.

"Perhaps he might like me to visit him, if such a thing were allowed?" I continued.

"You're a very kind young man, Tom," said Sir Ralph, weighing his words carefully. "It's what I've always admired in you. But may I give you a word of advice?"

"Of course," I answered.

"Don't be drawn into any of the King's little schemes, will you? What I've learned from my time under Cromwell is that His Majesty can't help

120

himself. He'll intrigue and plot, even when there seems to be nothing gained. He thinks he can play his enemies off against each other, Parliament, the army, the Levellers, the Scots, the French. He may try to use anyone who comes in from the outside."

I heard Sir Ralph, but I wasn't listening. I continued in my own train of thought.

"I think I'd like to explain myself, sir. For what happened after Naseby..."

"There's no need. What could you have done, as a mere boy against expert soldiers?"

He was right. We had been outnumbered and outwitted, of course, and I had scarcely been up to fighting weight. But I still felt the need to justify myself.

I wrote the letter. Two weeks later a reply arrived, delivered by a solitary rider on horseback, who waited while I read it, and then conveyed my answer back to the King. I was asked to come to the Spencer family house at Althorp on Wednesday week, where he had an appointment to play bowls.

I couldn't keep the news from Alice. That I'd be away a whole day, and that I was dressing for the occasion as well as I knew, made it obvious something extraordinary was happening. I couldn't think of a convincing untruth to cover my tracks.

"It's a strange sort of imprisonment," she began, "that allows the prisoner to be let out regularly to play *bowls*." It wasn't a game Alice understood, except as something old men did to waste time.

"It's a good game," I said lamely, "and I believe there is no bowling green at Holdenby."

"And he likes his games, doesn't he? Truly this king's played much with the fortunes of England." There was an edge in Alice's voice.

"I owe him a great deal," I ventured.

"Don't you owe us a great deal too?" she said testily. "If it hadn't been for my father, you'd be dead."

"That's perfectly true," I replied. "But it's also true that the King provided for me in Oxford when Dame Mary and I had next to nothing."

"I hope you don't have to choose between his affections and ours then," she snapped. What she meant was not "ours" but "mine". There was a growing understanding between us that our future might lie together as man and wife. It was unspoken, but we both knew it.

"I hope so too, Alice," I answered quietly, "but I must do this. Let's not fall out over it."

I only watched the King play, and wasn't invited to join in the game, for which I was very glad. With him were his gaolers, two of the commissioners for Parliament, Denbigh and Pembroke. They were both important men from the enemy camp, yet their attitude to the King seemed sympathetic. They were more like friends than accusers. It was also clear that they were regular competitors with each other and His Majesty, and as all three were highly skilled at bowls I'd have been outclassed. They seemed to have a knowledge of each and every blade of grass. This time the King triumphed and crowed over his success, though in life, as opposed to the game, Denbigh and Pembroke held the upper hand.

Afterwards, the King took me inside the house at Althorp. We walked its corridors, and he criticized its art collection.

"T-t-t-too gloomy," he said, writing off some dark views inside Dutch houses. "Far too s-s-stiff and f-f-formal" was his verdict on family portraits. "I knew *him* when I was young," he said, pointing at a figure dressed in doublet and hose, a huge man made larger by padded shoulders and puffed-out waist, "and he looked nothing like *that*!"

He asked me about Ashton, and my work. We smiled

about the time in Oxford. The subject moved on lightly to Naseby, and his views on Cromwell and Fairfax. He was unexpectedly generous.

"Cromwell's a g-g-g-great commander in the field," he remarked, "and so's Fairfax. Both good men, but Cromwell's the one to be feared. No understanding of art. Or wine. And he's got God completely wrong. He sees a fearsome judge, Thomas, whereas we must trust in a loving saviour. My comfort is that Cromwell will be more afraid to go to his death than I, when the time comes."

I tried to apologize for what I still thought of as my desertion of his cause. He waved me away. "You did your best, Thomas. No one can ask more."

"I feel I need your forgiveness, Your Majesty," I said hoarsely.

"Y-y-you *don't* need it," he replied rather sharply. "But if it's important to you, whatever there is to forgive is forgiven. By God as well as me."

He made me promise to visit again, and I was happy to say I would. Each time I saw him, we walked and talked about art and philosophy, and the countryside. At Holdenby, life wasn't unpleasant, just rather boring for him. He read a great deal, and rode every day, though he said the hunting wasn't much good.

"The deer in the forest at least know their king," he said disappointedly. "They stand to attention and ask to be dispatched. And where are the wild pig? All in the villagers' pots, I fancy."

He had a chapel to pray in, and a garden to walk in. He played chess. For a king who was used to excitement and ceremony, it was dull fare.

The fourth time I made the journey to see him, there came a moment when we were quite alone.

"I know you feel a little in my debt, Thomas," he said quietly.

I dropped my gaze instinctively.

"There may be a small thing you can do which would remedy the matter." He paused, significantly. "Will you do it, for me Thomas?"

"If it lies in my power, Your Majesty, of course," I answered, a trifle uncertainly, remembering Sir Ralph's warnings.

He thrust a thin package of documents at me, transferring it hastily from the inside of his jacket into mine.

"Make sure this reaches its destination," he whispered, glancing about him. "You'll s-s-s-see to whom it's addressed."

He looked me wolfishly in the eye.

"The slate's wiped clean, is it not?"

I should have felt pleased at this royal pardon, but its manner of deliverance and circumstances left me uneasy.

When I'd ridden clear of Holdenby, I pulled up my horse and inspected the contents of the slim package. The name to whom I was to take the bundle – Rawsthorne – meant nothing to me. Whoever he was, he lived at Buckingham.

Alice guessed what was up as soon as it became obvious I'd a journey to make shortly after my visit to the King.

"So what are you now? His spy, or his lapdog?" she asked scornfully.

"Neither," I said defensively, though when she mentioned the word "spy" I shivered inwardly.

The house wasn't hard to find, but handsome no more, set back from the road out of Buckingham in the direction of Brackley. I was received by a slight, bald man with a hooked nose. He spoke with a foreign accent, perhaps French. My heart missed a beat, and the word "spy" echoed in my head. The Queen was in France. Maybe this had some connection with her.

The Frenchman said he wasn't Rawsthorne, which was obvious enough, but assured me the package would be passed to him straightway.

"I should feel happier placing this in Master Rawsthorne's hands myself," I said doggedly. "It is from the King himself."

The Frenchman became agitated. "This I understand," he said in clipped tones. "It will be with him today."

"And how can I know that?" I said, withholding the letters.

"By my word," he hissed. I hesitated, and was amazed to see him loose the pistol from his belt. "I must insist," he added. "The letters, please! Now!"

I controlled myself as much as I was able. "There's no need for that," I said coldly, and handed the parcel over.

"Be assured, young man," was the mysterious stranger's parting shot, "we both serve the same master. All is well."

In my leaving I was of course disturbed about what had occurred, but there was no one I could confide in, Alice least of all, and having ridden uncomfortably back to Ashton, I kept my misgivings to myself.

I'd agreed I would visit the King once more, a fortnight later, on June 2nd. In those two weeks my anxiety steadily grew, and my temper was often short and unpredictable. Alice and I quarrelled frequently about small matters which should have been of no concern – whether the fish was cooked, or whether I had trodden mud into the house. In reality, I had started to see that my position was perilous, and begun to wonder if I had involved myself in an act which some might consider treason.

The rendezvous of the meeting was once more to be at Althorp and the plan was that I'd return with the King to Holdenby, there to spend a few nights at the house. I'd agreed with Sir Ralph that the estate could manage without me for a while. Alice scowled for days before I left.

She found me as I was saddling my horse for the journey.

"This matter will come between us," she pouted.

"Not on my part," I said.

"I wish he'd just go away," she said wistfully, meaning the King.

On the way to Althorp I turned over and over in my mind what my approach to His Majesty should be. Should I mention the Frenchman and my reception at Buckingham or not? In the event, the King's first words to me when we were alone were to thank me for the package's safe arrival.

"All is well then," I asked curiously.

"Y-y-y-yes, very well indeed," he said in a puzzled voice. "Should it not be so?" There was a pause. "You've rendered me considerable service," he said as we strolled around the beautiful rose-garden in the sunshine. I had not the courage to ask him what the service might have been, but as it turned out later that day, all was far from well.

In the early afternoon a game of bowls had been joined when a messenger rode in at a fair gallop. There was no ceremony. He came straight out with what he had to say to the King in front of the two old buffers, Denbigh and Pembroke.

"Armed horsemen are approaching Holdenby, Your Majesty," he said. "With what purpose, we do not know."

The King seemed unconcerned. He would have remained at his game of bowls. Denbigh and Pembroke were of a different mind.

"We must return, Your Majesty," said Denbigh.

The King laid a bowl to within an inch of the jack.

"At once, Your Majesty," said Pembroke firmly.

The King grimaced, but complied with their order.

It was a difficult situation. Naturally I didn't want to put myself in danger, but I also didn't want to show myself as a coward in front of the King. Since he thought the news of no importance, I supposed I had to treat it the same way, and I continued to Holdenby with them.

When we arrived, there was no sign of trouble. But after we'd gone to bed, at about midnight, there was a terrible commotion in the courtyard below. Looking out from the window it became apparent that the house was surrounded by a troop of horses, and that guards had been placed at every entrance.

I went down to the drawing room, pulling on my clothes as I did so. Pembroke and Denbigh were there before me. They looked distracted and anxious. Clearly, if there was a plot against Charles they weren't part of it, or else they were fine actors.

In the room with them was a man who looked to be no more than a common soldier, flanked by a half-dozen large and ugly pikemen.

"State your name and business," Pembroke was saying to the stranger. He spoke with less civility than seemed wise given that the visitors were armed, and we were not.

"My name's Joyce," said the leading man. "I'm pleased to be a cornet in Colonel Whalley's regiment. I regret I have no business with you, sir, only with the King."

Pembroke laughed contemptuously. "Then be on your way, if you value your life, Cornet Joyce," he said. "King Charles is in our safe keeping, and has nothing to say to Colonel Whalley."

At a nod, two of the strong-arm men took one threatening step forward towards Pembroke. The Commissioner's face clouded.

"This is no matter for debate, sir," said Joyce. He turned and pointed at me. "Where may I find King Charles's bedchamber?" he demanded.

"There are many rooms in the house," I said truthfully but unhelpfully, "and I've been here no more than five hours."

"Enough. Take me there, please," said Joyce to Denbigh.

Denbigh looked at Pembroke. He shrugged his shoulders resignedly. We were outnumbered. As Joyce said, there was little alternative but to obey.

Outside the royal bedchamber, Joyce knocked almost respectfully at the door. He'd left his guard behind, and had come alone. He seemed to have no intention of forcing his way in.

"Who goes?" came the reply from within.

"My name is Joyce, and I must speak with the King," the Cornet repeated. "Immediately!" he added firmly.

There was a further door beyond the one at which we stood. We could hear discussion between the King's attendants on the other side.

"Wait!" came the reply. Joyce seemed perfectly composed, but less so when a few minutes later he was told, "His Majesty will see you at dawn. The King will make his morning devotions and then receive you in the drawing room."

Joyce slapped his gloves on the opposite wrist in annoyance, but held his temper. "Very well, then! I shall await the King's pleasure," he said sarcastically.

While the King slept on, the rest of us waited for daybreak, wondering what it might bring.

A half-hour after dawn, the doors to the drawing room were flung open and the King's slight figure appeared in the doorway. Despite his small size, his presence still dominated the room.

Joyce cut straight to the point. "You're to accompany us, sir," he said. No "Your Majesty". No pleasantries.

The King seemed relaxed. "Am I indeed?" he said, seemingly almost amused by Joyce's lack of manners. "And what's your authority for this request? Why should I agree to your suggestion?"

Joyce walked to the window which looked out on the courtyard. He drew back the curtain. The courtyard was now full of smartly turned-out cavalry, well armed and ready to move. "There is my warrant, sir," he said simply.

King Charles went to the window and peered out. "Hmm," he said with a rueful smile. "It comes clearly written, without need of further spelling. So am I to travel alone?"

"These gentlemen should be company enough," said Joyce, sweeping his hand at Denbigh and Pembroke. "We need detain no one else. They may stay or go, as they please!" He looked at me as he said this.

The King caught Joyce's glance in my direction. By instinct he saw my anxiety that I was about to fail him, to desert him a second time. He addressed his next words to me in a kindly voice.

"Give it not a moment's thought, Thomas," he said. "Go and be a good steward to Sir Ralph Montagu and go with a quiet conscience. There's nothing you can do here."

Holdenby House was very quiet after the King and his small retinue had left to whatever fate awaited him, a huge building empty of purpose. I wandered its length for an hour or two, marvelling at its grandeur and elegance. Through the panes of its lovely windows I could see the rain lashing down mercilessly across the lawns and I had no wish to suffer an unnecessary soaking as I rode back to my duties at Ashton. I pondered what had happened and wondered again if my actions had contributed to the King's downfall. Try as I might, I could make little sense of the King's kidnap. He had been taken from the custody of his enemies by others who also claimed Parliamentary allegiance. Perhaps the army had now struck a blow against Parliament. Sir Ralph had reported mutterings that they believed themselves poorly paid. It seemed the King must now be considered a mere property to be bargained with.

Eventually the rain stopped and I took my horse from the stables into the Northamptonshire lanes at a slow and melancholy walk. Wherever the King was taken, he was now beyond my help or companionship. It was fully eighteen months before I was to see him again.

December 1648 – February 1649

It was Sir Ralph who told me shortly before the New Year of 1649 that the King was to be put on trial for treason. It took a few minutes for the news to sink in.

"There are those who think of the King as a boil to be lanced," said Sir Ralph. "They believe England's face will never be fair again until he's gone."

I looked through the window. England's face seemed anything but fair that December day. There was a nasty storm brewing and dead leaves were being harried around the bleak courtyard by a vicious wind. Food was short, and pestilence widespread. In the countryside the common people were struggling to survive, sometimes in vain. I had seen many buried before their time in the past few months.

"Are the sufferings of the poor the King's fault?" I asked wryly. "Or do others also carry a measure of responsibility for their plight?

Sir Ralph chuckled at the heat of my reply. "Easy, Master Thomas!" he said. "I'm only reporting what's said. I would not go to the stake for it myself!"

Sir Ralph sat himself heavily in his favourite chair by the window and sighed. "But the sovereign does not help himself, or his subjects, and that's plain. It seems he will never be quiet. I have it on the good authority of a commissioner that even from his prison cell at Carisbrooke Castle, he intrigues with France."

I shuddered at this echo from the past, and remembered uneasily my own brush with a mysterious Frenchman. What would Sir Ralph have thought if he knew I'd been part of such intrigues? I wanted to tell him, but could not.

Sir Ralph shook his greying head in disbelief.

"In consequence, his gaolers have so far discovered two plots against the King's life, and have themselves prevented his early death. Once, and I do not jest, they went so far as to dress His Majesty as an old woman. They smuggled him into a safe house until danger was past, and had the would-be assassins arrested. Now do you think we can begin to make a better life for England's citizens while such matters distract those who should be building prosperity?"

As a child I'd often thought how wonderful it might feel to be king and have complete control over everyone and everything. Now I thought, none of us are better off than leaves, kings included. We're all at the mercy of the wind of change.

"Anyway," said Sir Ralph gently, "I didn't wish you to hear later about the trial, or from other lips."

I considered a moment. "When and where will it be held?" I asked.

"January 20th. In Westminster Hall, London."

"Oh!" was all I could say. I was thinking how much I wanted to be there.

"*Go*, Thomas. With my blessing."

Sir Ralph had read my mind. He ran his finger along the dusty window ledge, and added as an afterthought, "Of course, this may not exactly be a *trial*. England without a king is like a body without its head. No wise man could possibly think it a good idea. Maybe it's Oliver Cromwell's notion to face the King with the truth. Perhaps he reasons that to be the greatest of all the King must learn to be the servant of all."

"Is the King like to change after all this time?" I asked.

"We must hope for the best, Tom, and for compromise and peace." Sir Ralph's face clouded. "But I have to warn you, there's another possible ending to this tale. Cromwell's in grim earnest, there's no doubt of that. I have heard his advisers speak of it, and Cromwell not Fairfax, is where true power lies now. If the King won't bend, he may be finally broken by that famous iron fist. If you go to London, bear it in mind."

Sir Ralph looked very hard at me, searching my face. "You understand my meaning?" he said.

I took a deep breath. "Would they openly dare to kill a king?" I asked.

"If they could show he carried enough guilt, and not enough humility," he replied.

I suppose I had some half-baked thought of riding into the capital and turning the King round, of being England's saviour. But such thoughts were fantasy.

For one thing I'd never been to the great city before, and was very shocked by its size and noise and crudeness. Once there, I immediately knew I'd have enough difficulty finding lodging for the night and Westminster Hall in the morning, without any thoughts of changing the King's destiny. I was all at sixes and sevens.

Sir Ralph had written on my behalf. Thus I had my place in one of the galleries they'd built around the hall especially for the trial. His letter of introduction said only that I was his steward, representing his interests. It mentioned nothing of my previous service to the King.

The hall at Westminster's a mighty work of craft. Imagine a timbered building nearly a hundred yards long, its roof criss-crossed with huge beams. All the public seats were full for the spectacle, and the mood of the crowd was hard to read. They weren't unruly, but not yet apparently happy with what was to take place. Voices were raised, faces surly. Fingers stabbed at the platform and at each other. The sound of the mob's conversation before proceedings began was an enormous grumble.

For one thing, the places where the commissioners were to sit on the platform were only half filled. These were the men appointed as judges over their sovereign, and yet many of the 150 had found more pressing things to do with their time.

A man in a neighbouring seat chortled at the sight of the empty seats. "Afraid to sign their names to a death warrant, are they?" he cried to those of us sitting near. "They wait to see which way the wind blows. Very sensible, I'd say."

Before the King arrived there was a strange intervention. As the commissioners' names were called one by one, they came to that of Sir Thomas Fairfax, the man who had for years pursued King Charles the length and breadth of the country, who in title at least had been Cromwell's superior officer. As his name was read out, an elegant woman sitting near me in the gallery rose from her seat and cried out passionately, "Not here. And never will be!" Her voice was heard all around the hall.

There was consternation. Heads turned to see who it was spoke so freely. But before she could be held for contempt of court, Lady Fairfax (for it was she) left the building in a flounce of skirts.

"Ooh, so Fairfax now leaves Cromwell's ship as well, does he?" commented my neighbour, rubbing his hands in glee.

I must have looked puzzled, for he explained himself to me further.

"Evidently the great Sir Thomas wishes no part of this play-acting. He has too much respect for the idea of a king, and quite right too!"

The King's entrance was dramatic. He appeared suddenly, walking with quick steps to his place before the judges at the southern end of the hall. He was dressed all in black, head to toe, and on his cloak the embroidered star of the Order of the Garter caught the light brilliantly. His hair was greyer than when I'd last seen him, and the beard a little more untidy, but his gaze was as direct as ever, his wit still as sharp.

As he reached his position, he looked about him pointedly at the empty seats, then slowly at the galleries. Did he see me among the crowd? There was a moment when I thought I caught a glimpse of recognition, before his eye moved on.

John Bradshaw, the President of the court, sat in the middle of them. There was nothing in his manner to suggest a leader of men. He spoke haltingly and in a low voice. He seemed to think as slowly as he spoke. He was only made remarkable this first day by a strange metal hat he wore, presumably for his better protection.

My loud-mouthed companion laughed coarsely when he saw it.

"Mr Bradshaw comes in fear of his life too, I see," he cackled. He swept an arm around the hall, indicating the pikemen arranged at its edges. "I think he has no need!"

The charge was read. There can have been no one in London who didn't hear the clerk thunderously lay the charge that:

"Charles Stuart, King of England, out of a wicked design to uphold in himself an unlimited and tyrannical

power, has taken away the right and power of frequent and successive Parliaments and has traitorously and maliciously levied war against the present Parliament and the people therein represented."

The charges went on to put responsibility for every cruel act of the last six years at the King's door. He was condemned as a tyrant, a traitor, a murderer and an enemy to the Commonwealth of England.

When he heard this the King shook his head, and laughed out loud.

"By whose authority am I brought here?" he asked after the clerk had finished.

Bradshaw answered ponderously, "In the name of the Commons of England assembled in Parliament, and all the good people of England."

It was an unequal contest between the two men. The King was quick on his feet, immediately in command of his audience, witty and assured. Bradshaw was dull and slow. His Majesty simply ran rings round him. He kept repeating his first question, each time picking on some small point to show that the court, such as it was, had no power to try him. The Commons hadn't been elected for eight long years. Whose views did they represent? Why were so many of them absent? And where were the members of the House of Lords?

Finally, his persistence really got under Bradshaw's skin. At the umpteenth repetition of the question, Bradshaw declared that he had the authority of the people of England on his side, of whom Charles was the *elected* king. Charles turned and looked very slowly around the great hall, up to the galleries where I sat, back down its length where the mass of common gawpers looked on.

"*Elected* king?" he said mockingly. "Since when was the king elected? These thousand years a king is a king by birth. Or at least until Mr Bradshaw now declares otherwise."

The day ended in uproar.

Nor was the second day of trial any better. At its close the court still had not heard the King plead guilty or not guilty. At one point a Colonel Hewson, one of the commissioner-judges, so far forgot himself as to rush forward from his seat spitting at the King and yelling for "justice". The hall, which had been a mess of noise at that point, went pin-drop silent.

The King wiped the spittle from his face very slowly with a silk handkerchief. When he'd finished cleaning himself, he looked Hewson straight in the eye and said firmly, "Justice awaits us all, sir, you and I alike. Nothing is more certain."

The court was adjourned until a third day. That night contradictory opinions raged back and forwards inside my head. At one time I'd think, "They can't convict him: there's no evidence and they have no authority." And then at another time I'd answer myself, "But he's so stubborn. He's so arrogant. They *must* have him done away with."

On the third day, there was a new mood in the court. Bradshaw and his cronies seemed to have a different plan and fresh resolve. They entered, more poker-faced than ever, to give the King a final chance to plead. He refused.

"If I were to acknowledge this court, sir," he said, "it would be a fundamental alteration to the laws of this land."

Bradshaw was ready for him. "How far you've preserved the fundamental laws of this land, and the freedom of the people, is shown by your actions. You've written your meaning in bloody letters throughout England." He paused for effect. "Clerk, record these words. And guards take him back whence he came! The court is adjourned."

For the first time, prevented from making argument, the King was visibly shaken. He was still attempting to speak as he was hustled away.

There *was* a hearing the next day, but it was behind closed doors, as the court heard from "witnesses" to the King's crimes. Who spoke for the defence, if anyone, I don't know.

The last Saturday, after a week of trial, the King was brought to Westminster one final time. If he was to offer terms, it would have to be now. The talk of London was that he might be willing to stand down as King, to abdicate in favour of Charlie, my one-time friend and his son. The hall was packed and on tenterhooks.

"May I speak, sir?" the King said as soon as he was walked up the steps to the platform in front of Bradshaw. It was the first time he'd begged permission – for anything. He sounded different. He was subdued, maybe defeated. The crowd was hushed, expecting some extraordinary event, either way.

"You'll have your chance to speak before judgement," Bradshaw replied. The King was caught off-guard. It was almost as though he'd not expected to be given the opportunity.

"I will?" he said.

"You will."

Two women with masks on their faces, as if dressed for a ball, stood and shouted from the gallery: "This

145

court's a sham. The charges are lies. The true tyrant is Oliver Cromwell." The whisper immediately went around the hall that one of them was once more Sir Thomas Fairfax's wife. The women were rudely dragged out by the soldiers, still shouting their protest. It was a moment when any strange event seemed likely.

But true to the last, when everyone expected the King to offer some olive branch to the court in exchange for his life, the speech he finally made was an arrogant appeal over the court's head.

He said he wished to be heard by Parliament in the Painted Chamber, away from Westminster and the crowds. He seemed to speak with reborn strength and as regally as I had ever heard him. Amongst his judges on the platform there was obvious disagreement. Some nodded their heads, others stood and waved their papers angrily, as if demanding his immediate dispatch to the scaffold. Finally, Bradshaw cut the argument dead and the commissioners withdrew, before returning a half-hour later to deny the King's request.

Charles made one final desperate throw of the dice, "I have a plan," he cried, "to put to the whole Parliament, for a lasting peace…"

But now the wagon was rolling, and it was too late to halt its path down the hill of destruction.

"Until you recognize us as a court, you will not be permitted to speak," intoned Bradshaw. "Clerk, read the sentence..."

To this very moment, I hadn't believed it would happen. A wave of rising panic seized me. My head was hot and swimming, my chest tight, my stomach churned. I scarcely heard what was said in its first part, but the final words have echoed in my head a thousand times: "*...for which reasons, this court adjudges that the said Charles Stuart shall be put to death by the severing of his head from his body.*"

The King struggled to speak, but the words wouldn't flow. For the first time in the trial, his stutter returned. He struggled to make a last declaration to the court as Bradshaw proclaimed with relish, and more style than he'd so far shown, "Guards, take him down."

I didn't want to go and see him die, but how could I stay away? They'd built the scaffold outside the Banqueting House in Whitehall, and very well too. As I passed by on a winter afternoon when the colour of the sky was the livid purple of a bruise, workmen were cheerfully planing and hammering perfection into a platform of oak planks. When they were done, they covered the scaffold in the finest black cloth. Truly it was a stage fit for a king.

The next morning I pushed my way through the drooling London mob into the space before the Banqueting House. I saw the King walk through its handsome windows and on to the platform. He came with absolute confidence, his head held high. He emerged as if to take the applause of his people, not as if his head was about to be split from his body. He was immaculately dressed as always, but now he seemed so very small. His porcelain-fine features had aged even in a few days. He looked closer to 70 than 50.

The crowd began to shift and murmur as he appeared, and the soldiers stood straighter and fingered their weapons.

I caught snatches of conversation in those who milled around me. Some in the crowd still believed Cromwell would show mercy. They thought there'd be a last minute reprieve, a pardon. Or perhaps they hoped a band of royal supporters would ride in and snatch the King away.

Some had revenge in their hearts. Like me they'd ridden or walked miles for the occasion. Unlike me, they were after blood for blood. They remembered the untimely death of a father, a son, a much-loved uncle and they blamed the King for it. *I* remembered Charles with gratitude as a man who'd been very kind. And I felt guilty that I'd failed him more than once. Above all I hadn't spoken out. I'd had my chances: before Naseby and then again at Althorp. Maybe if I'd done so, mere boy though I'd been, I might have persuaded him – to find a middle way, to be reasonable, to see the point of view of others.

I hadn't even had the chance to say goodbye. They'd let his children into St James's Palace to see him, but few others. Cromwell's men feared an attempt at escape too, even at this late hour.

Some other spectators thought, or perhaps only jested, that the act of killing a "divinely inspired" king would bring down a thunderbolt from the skies.

But there was no pardon. No thunderbolt. Just a bleak, most miserably cold of days, 30th January 1649.

The crowd was alive with rumours. It was said there'd been trouble finding an executioner. Who wants to be known for severing the head of the monarch? The authorities were clearly worried the King might struggle. They'd rigged up some kind of apparatus, all pulleys and levers, to drag him down on to the block if he put up a fight. As if he would! It seemed to me a last crude attempt at humiliating him, to make him seem like a wretched, cornered animal.

I stamped my feet in the bitter cold, and wished I'd more clothes to keep me warm. At last the drums started their death rattle and suddenly there he was, with the gentle Bishop Juxon on one side and a colonel on the other. The King carried a speech with him, but there wasn't the faintest chance it would ever be heard beyond the platform. The soldiers who flanked the scaffold had their instructions. Their baying, like so many mongrel dogs, drowned out his words.

Later I heard from a clerk of Juxon's that the King had fixed the soldier, a man called Tomlinson, with a steady gaze, and without a trace of his familiar stutter had summed up his view of life in a few short sentences, ending like this (I had the clerk write them down for me as a keepsake):

"Sir," he said, *"a subject and a sovereign are clear different things. It was for this that I now am come here and therefore I tell you that I am the martyr of the people. I have a gracious God."* He paused as if there was something else on his mind, but then simply added, *"I will say no more."* To Bishop Juxon he said the one word: *"Remember!"*

They pushed the King's mane of hair up under a linen cap, not unkindly. It was in everyone's interest for the axe's cut to be clean, the ending swift. He looked around him. Smiled to himself. Prayed earnestly, hands together, lips moving, eyes turned upwards. The executioners shivered and fiddled nervously with their masks as they waited for him to make ready. The occasional flake of snow fell from leaden skies.

At last the King nodded and they made him lie down for the block, despite his urgent requests that he be allowed to kneel. The chosen executioner raised his axe higher and still higher to the very point it must fall. Before it fell, I turned away and closed my eyes.

The awful groan and shudder of the crowd told me the deed was done. The murder. I think we should use the right word.

There was a tiny interval of shocked, stunned silence, before chaos broke out around the scaffold, and the mob grabbed what they could of cloth, wood, blood and chains, looking for souvenirs, until the pikemen stepped in.

Summer 1650

Alice Montagu has recently become Alice Adamson, and thinks it sounds well. We were married at the church in Ashton the Saturday after May Day.

England's master now is Oliver Cromwell, and Alice's father is a rising man in Northamptonshire. He was always moderate in his views, and his moderation has served him well.

Alice continues in her view that we have no need of a king at all. For my part, I think that in due course the people of England will have a second Charles on the throne, though he may not be a better sovereign than his father.

A Captain Baynes, late of the Parliamentary army, has bought Holdenby House for 22,000 pounds, and has set about demolishing the most beautiful house in England. He hopes he will make yet more money from the sale of dwellings he plans to build with the stone robbed from poor Holdenby, which now lies in ruins every bit as much as Grafton.

I'm weary of England and have developed a plan to

leave its shores for a better life. I'm told Virginia is a fine place, where there is as much land as a man could want. In a new country fortunes may be made honourably without petty squabbles and small-mindedness. I wonder whether Alice may be persuaded?

Historical Note

Imagine a present-day war in Great Britain which killed more than two and a half million of the inhabitants – at least one in 25.

In 1640 there were far fewer people living in the British Isles than there are now, but some historians have estimated that 250,000 lost their lives as a result of the battles that were to rage up and down Britain for more than ten years. Many were directly killed in the fighting (4,000 of the King's men at the Battle of Marston Moor alone!), and some died later because of their wounds. Besides these casualties, thousands of ordinary folk with little interest in the issues involved probably died from the poverty and disease which accompanied the English Civil War.

The War was a stop-start affair. Historians usually think of it as three separate wars, not one. Our story is mainly concerned with the first of the three, which lasted from 1642 to 1646. The last actually took place after the death of King Charles I. The first major event of the War was the Battle of Edgehill in October 1642 and the military conflict in England didn't end until 1652 when Parliament won a decisive victory at Worcester.

The roots of the War went back a whole generation. Charles came to the throne in 1625 after the death of James I, and throughout his reign there were rumblings of intrigue and discontent. The King's view was that his job, with God's help, was to make all the big decisions. He took England into expensive conflicts with Spain and France, and later with Scotland too.

Over ten years Charles sold off more than half a million pounds' worth of royal property (a huge amount, in present day terms!), but he still needed more money to pay for these badly managed expeditions. When he called Parliament together in March 1628, it was because he wanted them to vote to give him the cash he needed. He expected them to agree, simply because he was the King. However, Parliament had many complaints about the way government was being conducted – in particular, the forcing of loans on landowners, and the billeting of troops on civilians. They also wanted the King's commander, Buckingham, brought to account for his reckless actions in battle.

There was now an increasing number of independently wealthy and powerful men in the country, and they wanted to determine if and how their money would be spent. They believed Parliament should have the right to raise taxes, and not the King.

So when he didn't get what he wanted, the King shut down Parliament, and ruled entirely without it from 1629 to 1640. Charles managed to raise enough money during this time to keep England afloat. He levied taxes on goods going in and out of the country (this was called tonnage and poundage), and he first made ports and then later other towns pay "ship money" to finance the navy. All these moves were unpopular. Finally, when the war with the Scots went wrong, he was forced to recall Parliament to help balance the books. After such a long period away from power, Parliament's resentment at Charles' high-handed behaviour was unstoppable.

Behind these political differences of opinion lay a shifting fashion in religion. Puritan views were becoming more commonplace. With the coming of an English Bible, churchgoing had changed for ever. When services had been in Latin, ordinary people had to rely on the clergy for their understanding of the Christian faith. Now when they read or heard the New

Testament in plain English they found it made no mention of pomp and ceremony, of robes and incense. Instead, it seemed to talk about all men being equal. They began to want a plain, simple religion to go with the plain English.

The King had married a Roman Catholic, and his ideas of religion were old-fashioned – and not surprisingly, favourable to him! In his mind's eye, he probably saw a pyramid with God at the top, then the King underneath as God's earthly appointed representative, and finally, way below that, the mass of ordinary people. The King saw it as his duty to make them follow the inspiration he felt he'd received. If it meant imposing the Prayer Book on unwilling Scots, so be it.

Two wars with the Scots over the issue in 1639 and 1640 saw Charles' army humiliated, and ill-afforded money wasted. Through 1641 the tide started to turn against the King. London was in a state of turmoil and there were mobs on the street. Charles made the Viscount Strafford, his Commander-in-chief against the Scots, into a scapegoat. Despite a personal assurance to Strafford that he'd never come to harm, it was the King's signature which sent him to the scaffold, extracted under pressure from Parliament.

Eventually, in late 1641, the House of Commons declared that the King should only employ such counsellors and ministers as would be approved by Parliament, and that Parliament should be responsible for the defence of the realm. The King's power was ebbing away.

In the early days of 1642, the King left London for Hampton Court for his own and his family's safety, and both sides – the Parliamentarians and the Royalists – began to prepare for war.

The problem with understanding the English Civil War is that there's what one writer has called a "fact overload". The more you read about this period of history, the more complicated it seems to get. The story of Charles I is a great, simple, human drama – a tragedy, really. If Shakespeare hadn't been dead, he might have written a wonderful play about it. As Charles slowly lost his grip over the country he ruled, many other factions and individuals began to influence events. At times, everyone seemed to be plotting against everyone else, struggling for position, even among the Parliamentary ranks. Only very gradually did Oliver Cromwell emerge as the single strongest figure. That's why in this story we hear very little about him. Although the "New Model Army" –

the Parliamentary side's attempt at a co-ordinated, professional fighting force – was partly Cromwell's creation, Sir Thomas Fairfax was a much more important Parliamentarian figure throughout the period up to the King's death, which is why Lady Fairfax's outbursts at the trial were so shocking. Much as they disagreed with the King, few on Parliament's side believed that killing the King was the right thing to do.

Generally speaking, the events you hear about in this book really occurred and the locations are all factual. The house at Grafton Regis really was under siege and then burnt to the ground on Christmas Day 1643. Local legend has it that eleven people were killed in the drawing room rather than one, but there's no historical evidence to support it.

The battles that were fought in the years after the King formally raised his standard at Nottingham in August 1642 took place in just about every area of England. We know that some wealthy families were divided between support for the two sides. Sir Edmund Verney told his brother, Ralph, that he regretted they must now be enemies. Edmund was Knight Marshal of the King's Household while Ralph had declared himself for Parliament. In Yorkshire, Sir

Thomas Mauleverer had campaigned vigorously for Parliament and was later to sign the King's death warrant, but his son Richard was imprisoned because of his loyalty to the King.

Ordinary people suffered, as the people of Grafton did, because the War disrupted the rhythm of their lives. Men were recruited to the various armies, not always voluntarily, so their work had to be done by others, or it remained undone. The crime rate rose. Property was at risk of being looted. People were scared and demoralized.

If you live in Britain, there'll be a great story from the Civil War set somewhere near you. Go and find out about it, and ask yourself whose side you'd have been on, if you'd been living then!

Timeline

1600 A son, Charles, is born to King James I and his wife Anne.

March 1625 Charles is proclaimed King on the death of James I.

May 1625 Charles marries Henrietta Maria of France.

August 1625 Charles dissolves his first parliament when it places limits on the money available to fight a war with Spain.

1626 Buckingham arrested by Parliament. Parliament again dissolved by Charles.

1629 After disputes about the raising of money and religion Charles dissolves Parliament for a third time. It will not meet again for eleven years.

1633 Charles' choice, William Laud, becomes Archbishop of Canterbury. Laud is determined to unify the Church in England and Scotland under the English Prayer Book.

1634 "Ship money" – to support the Navy – raised from inland areas of England. This becomes another source of great resentment against the King.

1639 War with the Scots over imposition of the Prayer Book.

1640 Viscount Strafford and Laud press for recall of Parliament to fund Scottish war. When Parliament refuses, this "Short Parliament" is dissolved against Strafford and Laud's advice.

November 1640 Charles renews war with Scots. It fails and Charles is forced to recall Parliament yet again. (It's known as the Long Parliament.)

1641 Strafford executed. Laud imprisoned.

January 1642 King tries and fails to arrest five MPs. On the 10th January, Charles has to leave London.

August 1642 The King raises his standard at Nottingham and the Civil War proper begins.

October 1642 Battle of Edgehill. King advances towards London but is then held up. He spends the winter in Oxford.

1643 In a series of battles both sides win and lose military advantage by turns.

1644 Battle of Marston Moor is a disaster for Charles.

January 1645 New Model Army begins to form under Fairfax.

June 1645 Battle of Naseby. The Royalist army is routed. Besides the dead, a great number of prisoners are taken, and much equipment captured.

April 1646 Charles surrenders to the Scots at Newark in Nottinghamshire.

June 1646 Surrender of Oxford to Parliament.

February 1647 Scots hand over Charles. He's placed under house arrest at Holdenby.

June 1647 Cornet Joyce seizes the King at Holdenby.

November 1647 Charles escapes from Hampton Court to Isle of Wight, but is imprisoned there at Carisbrooke Castle.

November 1648 Charles is brought back to London by the army.

January 1649 Trial of King Charles I. He is executed in Whitehall on the 30th. The monarchy and the House of Lords are abolished.

1653 Having refused the offer of being made King, Cromwell is made Lord Protector of England. Now he has complete control.

1658 Oliver Cromwell dies.

1660 Charles II is restored to the throne.

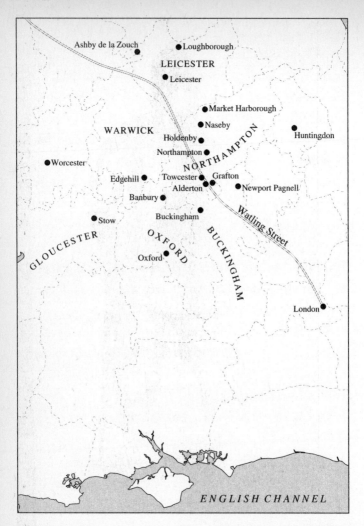

A map showing many of the places mentioned in this book.

A Roundhead general of Cromwell's Cavalry.

Try your match.   Guard your pan.   Present.

Give Fire.   Come up to your Musket.   Return your match.

Take up your rest.   Blow of your loose Powder and cast about your Musket.   Trail your rest & open your charge.

MUSKETEERS Pl. V.

A series of pictures of a soldier showing how to load, fire and carry a musket.

166

A triple portrait of King Charles I.

An engraving of Prince Rupert at the Siege of Leicester in May 1645.

The Effigies of the most Excellent & truly valliant S.r Thomas Fairfax Cap:tin Generall of the Armies raised for the preservation of Religion, defence of King Parlia:mt & Kingdome.

Lon: Printe   Peter Ster

Parliamentary general Sir Thomas Fairfax.

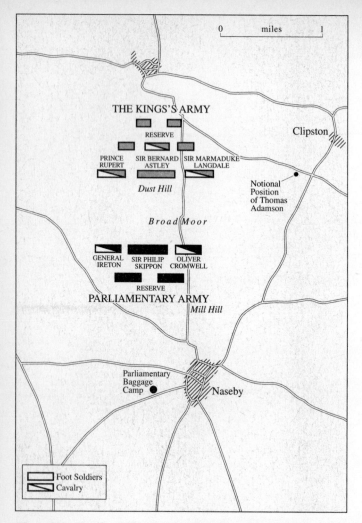

Plan of the Battle of Naseby showing the leaders of both army regiments.

A portrait of Oliver Cromwell.

King Charles I's death warrant. Note Cromwell's signature on the left.

Picture acknowledgements

P164 Map of Northamptonshire and surrounding counties, András
Bereznay

P165 A Roundhead General of Cromwell's Cavalry, Hulton Getty

P166 Musket drill, Hulton Archive

P167 Charles I in Three Positions (1600-49) Painting after Van Dyck
by Carlo Maratta or Maratti (1625-1713), The Trustees of the
Weston Park Foundation, UK/Bridgeman Art Library

P168 Siege of Leicester, Throsby, Engraved by Walker, Mary Evans
Picture Library

P169 Sir Thomas Fairfax, Mary Evans Picture Library

P170 Battle of Naseby plan, András Bereznay

P171 Oliver Cromwell, picture attributed to C de Crayer, Mary
Evans/Explorer

P172 Charles I's death warrant, Topham Picturepoint

TRAFALGAR

The Story of James Grant,
HMS Norseman 1799–1806

October 1805

The yards came round, spilling the wind from the sails,
and *Norseman* slowed to a standstill just out of range of
the enemy's guns, wallowing a little in the swell. More
and more of the ships in Lord Nelson's column were
coming up in turn to add the weight of their gunfire to
the fray. Beyond, I could see the ships of Admiral
Collingwood's column similarly engaged. It was a
tremendous spectacle that almost made me forget the
task I had been given. I looked towards the front of the
enemy line and, sure enough, five of their ships were
turning slowly and heading back towards the fighting…

THE TRENCHES

The Story of Billy Stevens, The Western Front 1914–1918

June 1917

Mustard gas! A feeling of panic hit me and I scrambled to get my respirator over my face before the killer gas got into my mouth and nose and burnt my lungs. It burned everything it touched. Eyes. Skin. And it always found a way in. Like now, I could feel where it had crept up inside the sleeves of my uniform and the skin on my arms felt like it was on fire. I threw myself into a muddy hole, pushing my arms under water, but I knew it was already too late. I stumbled to my feet, saturated, with the weight of wet mud clinging to me. I couldn't move.
I couldn't see...

BATTLE OF
BRITAIN

THE STORY OF HARRY WOODS,
ENGLAND 1939–1941

October 1940

I was out, free of my aircraft, tumbling wildly in the air.
I pulled the ripcord. I was jerked back by the parachute
as air punched into it and I swung there like a puppet,
winded and gasping for breath. I looked down at my leg.
It felt like a bear was gnawing on it but it was still in one
piece. For now, anyway. Then I heard it – right behind
me. An Me109 diving towards me, guns blazing. There
was nothing I could do. Nowhere I could go. Shells
whistled past me on either side. I just thought, OK then.
If this is it, OK. Maybe my turn had finally come…